"You saved my life," Mallory said.

"I want to help save yours by helping you catch this guy. You know, return the favor."

Shamus took Mallory's elbow and moved her to a corner away from everyone else. "I have a couple of ways you can return the favor," he said slowly. "They are really important to me."

Her eyebrows raised in question. He continued, "Promise me you will *not* get involved in this bombing investigation. And that you won't invite me to join the other probation officers at lunches and after work anymore. I don't want to be a part of things."

Her reaction was the same as if he'd taken a rose and crushed it under his heel. His heart thumped painfully. He *had* to be this way.

"You are such a hard man to like," Mallory told him. "But I'm not giving up on you."

Books by Florence Case

Love Inspired Suspense

Deadly Reunion
Mistletoe and Murder

FLORENCE CASE

is a New Jersey native who expected to stay in the Northeast to work, and so earned a bachelor of arts degree in German from Montclair State College (now University). Then she met and married her fantastic husband and moved to the Deep South, where she has run into only one person who spoke German. But her college education was not wasted—she had several novels published before coming to Steeple Hill to write; she homeschooled her beloved son, born with autism and developmental delays, for several years; and she's trying hard to get another B.A. in speaking Southern. Because she loves to knit sweaters, crochet for babies in need, and teach adult Sunday School, most never suspect Florence dives right into danger—she once went after a really big snake in her front yard with her really little car. All kidding aside, the only danger she dives into is in the stories she makes up in her head and the ones she reads in other romantic suspense novels, which she loves. You can catch up with her latest news on www.shoutlife.com/FlorenceCase.

MISTLETOE and MURDER

FLORENCE CASE

Steeple
Hill®

Published by Steeple Hill Books™

STEEPLE HILL BOOKS

Steeple
Hill®

Recycling programs
for this product may
not exist in your area.

ISBN-13: 978-0-373-44363-5

MISTLETOE AND MURDER

www.SteepleHill.com

Printed in U.S.A.

Let all bitterness, wrath, anger, clamor, and evil speaking be put away from you, with all malice. And be kind to one another, tenderhearted, forgiving one another, even as God in Christ forgave you.

—*Ephesians* 4:31–32

My brethren, count it all joy when you fall into various trials, knowing that the testing of your faith produces patience.

—*James* 1:2–3

To Jessica Miller and Jack Phillips, the kids of my heart, for keeping me laughing all the time, but especially in October. And thanks to Eric— any mistakes are mine.

Special thanks to Melissa Jeglinski and Tina Colombo, for their understanding and kindness.

ONE

Finished with her pre-sentence report, Mallory Larsen picked up a box wrapped in shiny red and silver Christmas paper and turned a speculative gaze on the only other probation officer left in the office past closing time on a Friday—Shamus Burke. She'd give making friends with him one last stab, and if a present given from the heart didn't work, she was done trying.

Shamus rarely spoke unless he had to, and his stare was so intimidating their coworkers avoided him whenever possible. No one had minded when he'd skipped out on the Christmas party earlier that afternoon. No one except her. Because he hadn't used to be so mean.

On the contrary. A couple years back, the former police detective had really enjoyed the Christmas season—at least from what she'd seen while he and his wife participated in the church's Christmas cantata along with her. He'd always been friendly with other church members and happy to visit with residents at the nursing and assisted-living homes where they'd sung. His love for the Lord had radiated from him.

As had his love for his wife. They'd had the kind of relationship Mallory had always yearned for. She'd admired him from afar, and wished for a man like Shamus to come into her life.

But then he'd dropped out of church—and out of sight—

to catch his wife's murderer. When he'd resurfaced again as Mallory's coworker at the Shepherd Falls County Probation Office a month ago, all traces of the old Shamus were gone. He'd acknowledged remembering her but then had been tense and uncommunicative and a royal pain to all of them, and she wanted to see the old Shamus back. This new one was just too hard to live with.

Gift in hand, she rose and walked right by the sparkly Christmas cards edging the desk of her best friend, Ginny Keane, but couldn't resist stopping at Mosey Burnham's workspace to press the top of his cherry-cheeked, tabletop Santa's head.

"Ho, ho, ho!" the Santa called out, which made her grin and got Shamus's bent, black-eyed gaze pointed in her direction, one eyebrow lifted.

Oops. So much for ambushing him so he wouldn't have a chance to think of an excuse to refuse her gift. His eyes narrowed as she reached his desk, which was the only one in the room that didn't have anything Christmasy on it. Sad, considering this was the same man who once sang in the cantata performance wearing a small Santa pin. Shamus needed *help*. Giving him her most cheerful smile, she held out the present.

"Merry Christmas," she said.

He didn't reach out or nod his head. He just stared. Which wasn't a bad thing, necessarily. With his black, wavy hair, thick eyebrows and the crinkled corners of his black-velvet eyes, he was awfully easy to look at.

Too bad he wasn't as easy to deal with.

No matter. He was getting the gift whether he wanted it or not. She could be stubborn, too, if it were for someone's own good.

"You missed the Christmas party earlier. I brought a handmade gift for everyone, and this one's yours." The silver, scissor-curled ribbons on top bounced as she presented it again.

For a few seconds, his eyes flickered with some emotion she couldn't quite catch, but then the intense stare was back. His shield.

"I didn't stay for the party on purpose," he said.

"I realized that when you came back after you thought everyone had gone home and scowled when you saw me."

"I didn't scowl," he denied.

"You *always* scowl." She wiggled the present in front of him, but he didn't reach for it. "You do it to scare people off."

The edges of his mouth almost turned up, but he caught himself. "How come it doesn't work with you?"

"Because the only person who scares me is my mother and her plans to get me to move back home." She flashed him another big grin. He merely continued to stare at her as if that hint of a smile had never happened.

Her grin faded.

"Your scowls don't work on me," she told him, "because I don't give up on most people that easily. That amazing trait is why I'm in this line of work."

She laid the box down at the side of his desk. "If you're shy, you can take it home with you to open. I don't mind. I just wanted to make sure you weren't left out."

He didn't say anything. She wasn't about to let his silence intimidate her, but she felt so awkward standing there. His total lack of response to her gift made her feel stupid for trying to be kind.

Turning, she walked back near her desk to get her coat from the rack. What she'd said was true—she didn't give up on people easily. But in Shamus's case, four weeks of invitations and being her usual sunny self hadn't worked. It was time to quit. She knew from sad experience that there were some people who needed to wallow in their misery, and the last thing she was going to do was join him. Not her. She'd lived in a house of misery growing up, but she'd gotten out, discovered the Lord and joy in her life, and become happy.

She was determined to stay that way.

Great. Not only was he contented with being miserable, now he was dragging others into his pit. Shamus typed another sentence describing a probationer's part-time job, but he was distracted. Mallory Larsen had a rep, at church and here, for doing good that came straight from her heart. Her eyes were practically begging him to be happy. She deserved a thank-you at the very least. The only thing holding him back was that he didn't want to give her the impression her gift had made the least bit of difference in his life. It hadn't.

But that wasn't her fault. Nor was it the Christmas season making him like he was. It was just the total lack of joy in him since what felt like...forever, but had only been a year and six months, give or take.

He should have figured Mallory wouldn't go home early. Not because she was a workaholic, but because she cared about her probationers and worked overtime for them. Him? He honestly had nothing else to do, and with each of the six probation officers in Shepherd County, Indiana, carrying almost two hundred cases, the department had an endless stream of work. He might as well get some of it done.

Sitting back in his chair, he watched Mallory shrug on a beige coat with a fur collar over her red sweater and white slacks. She pulled her long, chestnut-red hair free from her collar and let it fall over her shoulder. One lock fell near a sparkling Christmas-wreath pin to the right of the fur.

Funny how he'd stopped being able to concentrate on his work the second she'd pressed down on the Santa's head and laughed, but he could focus just fine on her. Well enough to see every detail of her clothing, hair and face. And well enough to see how fast her cheerful smile had faded when he hadn't laughed at her joke and refused to take her gift.

He asked God once more to help him change his attitude, right then and there. His faith made him keep praying, even though he didn't think it would do any good. He'd come to believe after his wife's murder that the Lord wanted him to suffer for a while.

God didn't seem any more friendly, either, by the time Mallory left her desk, heading toward the front office door, which was kept locked to offer the officers some protection from the riffraff—uh, make that *probationers*—they served. The look on her delicate features was gloomy compared to her normal, smiling face, and he couldn't stand it anymore. If God no longer cared about his life enough to answer his prayers and truly change his heart, then he would have to pretend.

"Mallory?" he said as she turned the dead bolt on their office door.

Her hand paused as she turned her head to look at him, hope lighting her eyes.

"Thanks," he said with a nod. "For thinking of me." He still didn't care that she had, but acting was a valuable trait for a detective, and he'd learned it well.

Her lips curved upward, but her eyes dimmed with suspicion. She was seeing right through his insincerity, but at least he'd tried. It was the best he could do.

Opening the door, Mallory walked through and left it to shut on its own. Shamus barely had enough time to remind himself once again what a louse he was when he heard a startled shout and a grunt outside the door.

Mallory. No one should be in that hall. Muscles tightening, he drew his weapon and rose, just as Mallory was propelled through the almost closed door back into the room by a man who had a Smith & Wesson pointed at her head.

* * *

This couldn't be happening. In less than three seconds, Mallory had gone from a tiny bit of progress with the icy Shamus Burke to being held hostage by...whom? She recovered enough to look sideways at the man who was holding her arm in his shaking fingers.

Her mouth dropped open. Bud Tripp? Meek, mild-mannered accountant Bud Tripp, who had stolen a thousand dollars from his employer to move so he could get his teenage daughter away from bad influences, and had even been paying it back when the theft was discovered? If the gun hadn't been real, she would have thought someone was playing a really bad joke on her.

"Mr. Tripp, what on earth are you doing?" She yanked out of her probationer's loose grasp and faced him. The man, in his early fifties, was flushed red, perspiring heavily and shaking with fear or maybe cold. His jacket was too thin for the icy air outside, and his awkwardly fitting ball cap didn't look very warm, either. His dress slacks were soaked at the bottom, probably from snowdrifts. He had a backpack on his back that looked stuffed. If it contained his possessions, maybe he'd been evicted from his new rental home and was having a mental breakdown.

That would explain everything. Which would be nice, because she definitely had no clue what he was doing.

"Put down your weapon, Tripp!" Shamus ordered, moving out from behind his desk, his department-issued Glock pointed at the smaller man.

Mallory's eyes darted to Shamus, whose hands were a whole lot steadier than Tripp's. "The gun is unnecessary, Shamus. Mr. Tripp doesn't want to hurt us." Her voice was sharp, and she instantly regretted it. She wasn't like that. She'd never be like that. Softening her tone, she added, "But you're so sweet, trying to protect me."

"I was a cop for ten years. It's what I was trained to do," Shamus told her between gritted teeth, his gaze never drifting from the gun Tripp held. "And I am not sweet."

"Heroic, then," Mallory said. She meant it. No man had ever tried to protect her like that. She liked it.

Shamus just scowled, and so she turned back to Tripp. She wasn't afraid. She had a natural instinct about people—even a judge had told her that once—and Bud Tripp was not a killer. She had gotten to know him on her last home visit with him. Good thing it was just last week. With all the probationers she had to keep track of, she might not have remembered the man otherwise—that's how safe and normal Tripp was. She didn't have any idea why her probationer was doing this, but she honestly didn't believe he would hurt her.

Shamus hurting Tripp, though, she wasn't sure about. Her instincts were all out of whack when it came to the former detective.

"Mr. Tripp," she said, keeping her tone as authoritative, yet low-key, as possible, "please put that gun down. I know you don't want to harm anyone, and I would hate it if you accidentally hurt yourself."

"I, on the other hand, wouldn't lose any sleep over it."

Shamus's intimidating words worked. Tripp swung his gun downward, and Mallory sighed with relief.

"Ms. Larsen is right about me," Tripp said, his voice squeakier than Mallory remembered. He focused on her. "And she's a really kind person—"

"Yeah," Shamus broke in. "We'll put that on her tombstone. She was a kind person, and it got her killed."

Oh, this was so not the man she'd been acquainted with, and admired, two years ago. That man would never have put anyone down like that. Mallory pursed her lips. Apparently Shamus thought she was a fool for trusting Tripp...or for being nice in general—she wasn't sure which. Either way, for some reason, his criticism hurt.

"That's it, Shamus," she said. "You're officially off my Christmas gift list for next year."

His stern gaze flickered with what looked like disappointment to her. She must be seeing things.

"Don't criticize Ms. Larsen," Tripp ordered Shamus, shifting his weapon back toward him.

Shamus didn't respond, just kept his own weapon pointed straight at Tripp, his wide shoulders steady. No negotiations possible with Shamus Burke, it looked like. Okay. That just meant she'd have to defuse the situation before Shamus took action, so no one would get hurt.

She refocused on the former accountant.

"Let's pretend he's not here, Mr. Tripp," Mallory said, doing away with authoritative and trying soothing. "Tell me what's wrong. Tell me how I can help you." She beckoned for his weapon, but Tripp raised his free hand.

"You two have to leave," he said. "The building has to be empty."

"Why?" she asked, drawing out the word. Her subdued manner seemed to be working, judging by the way some of the fear had left Tripp's voice, and his shoulders had slumped. But then, to her right, she sensed Shamus stepping forward.

"Drop the weapon, Tripp!" he ordered again.

Shamus was *definitely* getting on her nerves. Mallory took a deep breath to keep herself from saying something not so nice. She was a Christian and needed to show Shamus some understanding. He didn't know her at all. He had no idea she was capable of handling this on her own.

The first step was to make Shamus see Tripp as a human being. She said a quick prayer under her breath and then turned to him. "Shamus, please," she said. "Can't you see he's scared to death?

"That makes two of us," Shamus said.

"You?" she asked. "Frightened? I don't believe it."

"Yeah, I'm scared he's going to end up killing you." Shamus took another step forward. Tripp backed up to where he could see both of them at once, arcing the gun back and forth nervously.

"Please don't try to stop me!" he said. "This man—he says he took my daughter, and if I don't do this, he'll kill her."

"Somebody took Tara?" Mallory's heartbeat revved up with her first real flush of fear. Tara Tripp was a sweet teenager who liked to read. She reminded Mallory of herself at that age. And now she was in the clutches of some nut who was sending another victim to do…whatever it was Tripp was supposed to do? Her fear started to turn to anger, and she quickly squashed that down.

Retreating, she stood next to Shamus, whose expression never lost one bit of its fierceness. In the light of the new information about the kidnapping, that fierceness now was comforting.

Not that she would admit it to him.

"*Who* has Tara, Mr. Tripp?" Mallory asked.

"Just leave so I can get on with it," Tripp pleaded. "Please?"

"Get on with *what?*" she asked him, truly perplexed.

"He has a bomb in the backpack," Shamus said matter-of-factly, as though he'd known it all along and it didn't terrify him one bit. Her? Her eyes felt like saucers. She blinked, hard, as her gaze shot back to Shamus. He wasn't joking. His eyes were narrowed and shadowed, his full lips in a thin line. He looked ready to pounce.

And she was almost ready to let him.

No denial sprang from Tripp about the bomb, so Shamus

had to be correct. A thin sheen of sweat on her brow joined her thumping heart.

"You need to leave, Mallory," Shamus said softly, in a different tone than she'd ever heard from him before.

She wanted to. The only thing stopping her was extreme doubt that the caustic Shamus would get any information out of Tripp at all. Her coworker might not like it, but he needed her there.

"Do you have any idea who this kidnapper is or where he might be holding your daughter?" she asked Tripp.

Tripp just stared at her.

She persevered. "Do you have a contact number? Do you know why he's doing this?"

"No." Tripp shook his head. "No to everything."

"The police can help you, Mr. Tripp. We need to call them," she said. With a trembling hand, she reached for Shamus's phone, the nearest one.

"He says get away from the phone!" Tripp yelled.

Startled, Mallory dropped the receiver onto its base and took a quick step back, bumping into Shamus. His arm slipped around her waist, steadying her. A few seconds of his touch was reassuring, but it was probably good he withdrew his arm—since they were in the middle of maybe getting blown up and all.

"Who said get away from it, and how would anyone but us know what I was going to do?" she asked.

Shamus spoke. "Tripp sometimes delays answering you. I think he's wired for sound and possibly has a video cam on his jacket or the backpack strap." He paused. "Isn't technology wonderful?" He sounded weary, almost as though none of this was surprising him, and he was sorry that it didn't.

"We should leave, then," she said.

"I think I just said that a minute ago." He indicated the rear exit with a sweep of his head. "Go."

She should leave. She wanted to. But she felt a strong tie to this man—the first person who had ever tried to protect her from harm. Why wasn't he budging from his spot to save himself? Probably he wanted to stand guard over Tripp so she could get out of the building safely. No matter what his reason, Shamus was the bravest person she'd ever seen, and she couldn't abandon him. She just couldn't let him face this danger alone.

"I'm not leaving without you," Mallory said. Of course, that made her officially insane.

The look Shamus shot her made her think he'd read her mind and agreed.

"Tell you what," he said, his hands still holding his weapon. "If you go, you can take that present on my desk with you for safekeeping, and I'll let you give it to me again later."

He wanted her gift. The pleasure she felt over that, unfortunately, was curbed by the danger they were in.

She picked up the wrapped box. "Come with me, Shamus, and you can open it outside." How innocent that sounded. Like they would be going outside for a party instead of escaping a bombing. She swallowed down her terror.

He didn't move.

"You have to come with me," she told him, her voice growing unsteady. There was no real reason for him to stay…unless he didn't care about his life. She gazed up at him. That couldn't be it.

Panic joined her fear. Her heartbeat made her think of the hidden timer that could be on the bomb, and go off anytime. She didn't fear dying—she just wasn't ready. There were things she wanted to do first.

Like save Shamus from himself.

"Let's go, Shamus," she said, using her authoritative tone.

Shamus shook his head. "I can't. You heard Tripp. The building is supposed to be empty. As long as there's someone here, he can't blow it up. I'll stick around and save the tax-payers some money."

"You're kidding, right?" she asked, her heart falling when he didn't respond. "Or do you have a death wish?"

For a few long seconds, Shamus met her gaze. Not a death wish. Too much defiance was in the dark depths of his eyes. But she *was* getting the impression he just didn't care about his life. She would ask him why, but he couldn't tell her, not with some madman listening via Tripp.

"They won't go!" Tripp said, apparently talking to whoever was at the other end of his microphone. "They're crazy. Neither of them will go."

"We're crazy?" Mallory and Shamus asked together, and then glanced at each other, startled at the coincidence. Too quickly, Tripp started moving, a sharp reminder to Mallory to stop focusing so much on the office recluse.

"You both have to leave *now*," Tripp ordered, backing up and over to the wall, allowing them plenty of room to leave without getting close to him via the front door. He brandished his weapon. "Now! He said you'd better hurry."

"Mallory, get out of here," Shamus said fiercely.

Mallory's stomach clenched harder. But she couldn't leave Shamus alone. She didn't even know why, but she couldn't.

Shamus's arms never wavered as he kept his gun pointed at Tripp. Where did he get the strength? Her whole body was shaking.

"Ask the guy, Tripp," Shamus said, "what happens if I don't leave?"

"Please," Tripp begged. "He says he's going to kill my daughter. He says he'll prove it."

The phone chirped on Shamus's desk, startling Mallory so badly she jumped right into the side of him. He lowered one arm long enough to grab her hand and squeeze it gently. His fingers were warm, his touch calming. She wanted to keep holding his hand and go into denial.

The phone rang again, but the idea of talking to someone who was threatening them by holding a teenage girl hostage overwhelmed her to the point she couldn't move.

Go into denial? She was already there.

"Pick it up!" Tripp ordered. "It's *him*."

Stepping sideways to the phone, Shamus answered it, hit the speaker button and took his gun again in two hands. "Look, you—"

"Daddy!" The voice of Tripp's daughter wailed over the speaker. "Come get me!"

They heard a slap that Mallory felt through her cheek and into her bone. She slammed her eyes shut, remembering another abduction, long ago. How helpless she'd felt not being able to do anything...

Tara's scream cut through the air, and Mallory opened her eyes. This was not happening to *her*—it was happening to Tara. She couldn't do anything then, but now she could get a grip and help this girl.

"Tara, it's Mallory, your father's probation officer," she said toward the speaker. "Don't be scared. I promise I will help you. No matter what." Somehow. And she could only pray she'd be able to keep that promise.

The phone went dead.

Mallory's eyes flew to Tripp. He was leaning against the wall, on the verge of collapse. His daughter was sixteen. Mallory figured he loved Tara tremendously—he'd risked everything to steal money to get her away from bad influences at her old school. He'd broken the law and needed to be punished and finish making restitution, yes, but a part of Mallory admired him and wished her mother had been brave enough to get her and her brother out of the situation they'd been in.

But she needed to stop thinking about her past before she had no future.

Tripp's knees gave out, and he sank to the floor. "He's going to hurt Tara! She's all I have."

Shamus started toward Tripp again, with Mallory right behind him. She didn't get three steps before Shamus put up his arm as a barricade and forced her to stop.

Tripp was picking himself up, his weapon once again pointing outward. "Can't sit," he said, wiping his forehead with the sleeve of his jacket. "Blocks the camera view. He has to see when Burke leaves."

Shamus was specifically mentioned, but not her. This attack *was* about Shamus. *She* was obviously expendable.

But why? What was going on? If it was about Shamus, then why was her probationer involved?

"You're not leaving?" Tripp asked, sounding desperate.

Mallory didn't take her eyes off Shamus, who shook his head negatively.

"Then I have to. He says abort the mission. Please don't follow me. My daughter won't be safe if you do." Still pointing his weapon at them, Tripp edged swiftly to the door, opened it and hurried through, leaving the two of them alone in the room.

"I need to go after him," Mallory said, but Shamus beat her to the door and threw the deadbolt.

"Go out the back," he whispered close to her ear.

"Why?" she asked, whispering back. "You heard him. The bomber told him not to go through with it."

He grabbed her hand and pulled her toward the rear of the huge office. "I'm not sure I believe Tripp, and bomb or no bomb, whoever it is will be expecting us to come out the front. I don't like that idea. Hopefully, it's only one person, and there's no one waiting in back. We'll call the police outside."

"You didn't hit the alarm?"

"What alarm?" he asked, looking frustrated.

Yanking out of his grasp, she double-timed it to her desk and stuck her foot under it. "Under our desks. They probably didn't install yours yet."

Now someone tells him—*after* the emergency starts. Shamus grabbed his present from her so she would have her arms free to run and went to the door in the back that connected the receptionist's office to theirs.

Opening it, he saw the adjoining office was clear. So was the bulletproof receiving window at the very front of the room that showed part of the hallway through which Tripp had exited. Shamus strode four feet to the exit door, yanked it open and surveyed the parking lot. No signs of anyone lurking in wait. He hoped he was right.

He turned to motion for Mallory.

She wasn't there.

Shamus cursed and reached the inside door just as she got there, clasping the laughing Santa from Mosey Burnham's desk. She paused in place when she saw the fury on his face. Did she have a death wish?

"The Santa belonged to Mosey's daughter. She was killed in action," she explained quickly. "It's all he has left of her."

"Items can be replaced—people can't."

"I know. I'm sorry. I guess my heart gets in the way of my thinking sometimes."

She sounded so sincere that Shamus considered apologizing for his abruptness. No time. Turning without responding, he strode to the door and stepped out onto the welcome mat. He hoped he was wrong about Tripp's leaving the bomb behind. Hoped they had all the time in the world to get out of the building. Hoped—

The air around him exploded.

TWO

The force slammed Shamus upward and away from the building, sucking the breath out of him. He hit the snowy asphalt a few feet away and lay there, stunned, as all the emotion he'd buried since his wife's death tumbled back onto him along with the debris from the bomb. Emotion over another woman.

Mallory.

Did she make it? He pushed himself onto his knees. Swiveled around to face the building. His head spun. He made himself focus, but he didn't see her. She had to still be inside.

Annoying, do-gooder Mallory, who just *had* to stay late to give him a present so he wouldn't feel left out. Who couldn't believe her client could actually hurt someone. Who wouldn't leave him behind even though she'd had the chance…

He had to rescue her. He could not have another woman's death on his conscience.

Finding his gun on the ice, he holstered it, then lunged toward the building. At least, his muddled mind thought he was lunging, but he was startled to find he was only limping slowly. No matter. He pushed onward, trying to move faster, his ears ringing and his head spinning when he tried to turn it.

Sucking in a deep breath of clean air, he plunged inside the doorway and found a dazed Mallory against the outer wall, clutching Mosey's Santa. Fire licked at what was left of the wall near the receiving window. Smoke poured into the area. Get her out. He had to get her out.

Fighting the stars that threatened to push him into darkness, he lifted her into his arms and carried her outside into the parking lot and away from the swirling smoke and dust. She didn't speak, not one word, and something inside him—he wasn't going to call it his heart—clenched.

His wife hadn't spoken when he'd found her, either. She was already dead.

When he was far enough from the building to be safe, he picked a dry spot on one of the cement parking blocks near an overhead light post and sank down on it, keeping her in his arms and ignoring the ache in his knee.

Sirens whined in the distance.

He looked down into her heart-shaped face. Her eyes were closed, but she still gripped the Christmas toy she'd considered worth her life.

"Mallory!" he called to urge her awake, loudly because he could hardly hear and figured she was at least as bad off. He had to make sure she'd be okay in case he passed out. "Mallory, open your eyes."

She did. They were deep, sea-green eyes, he saw in the lamplight. He'd seen them before, of course, but he had purposely not noticed their color. Not noticed anything but how they smiled when she smiled. Didn't want to notice now.

But he did.

"You saved me," she said. She covered one ear and frowned. "I can't hear."

"What?" he asked her.

"You saved me," she said again, louder, and coughed with the effort. Her lips lifted in a gentle smile that gifted him more than any present she could give him. She took a breath and said loudly, "I owe you."

"No, you don't," he said just as loudly. He didn't want anyone to owe him, especially not a woman like Mallory. "I saved you for a purely selfish reason. So you don't owe me anything."

"What reason?"

Oh, great. Now he had to hurt her again, because he wasn't lying. Everything he did lately was for selfish reasons.

"I would have to take a bunch of your cases over if you ended up in the hospital, and I'm overworked as it is."

The smile left her lips, and she shut her eyes again. Wonderful. That was why he didn't get involved with people anymore. He just hurt them, and he couldn't seem to stop.

The regret that he'd tried his best to bury burned once more in him. But if he made amends, she might get the idea he wanted to be friends. He didn't. All he wanted was to be left alone.

Stop thinking, he told himself. Shut down. Observe. Watch for anyone who looked familiar, who might be behind the bombing. Protect Mallory from him. Since he'd spent years in the Shepherd Falls Police Department, being on guard was easy to do, and much better than actually feeling anything.

People gawked from the parking lot across the street, probably too afraid of another explosion to come closer and offer help. He searched their faces, hoping to see someone he'd arrested in the past who might want to kill him. But the growing darkness made it difficult to see into the shadows. Actually, he and Mallory were the ones in the light—from the overhead safety lamps the city had installed to keep the probation officers safe.

The irony of that didn't escape him. He was a sitting duck.

Fire and rescue screeched around the corner as Shamus watched, followed by police cars, their flashing red-and-blue lights adding to the red-and-green Christmas ones decorating the Shepherd Falls business district.

"Help me stand up, Shamus," Mallory said, jolting him. He'd thought she'd passed out. With some relief that she had survived the blast better off than he'd thought, he helped her to her feet. She was wobbly, but remained upright as the paramedics pulled up nearby.

"I'll fill in the police. You go to the hospital," he told her, hoping she didn't try to argue with him.

She didn't. Instead, she held Mosey's Santa out with both her trembling hands. "I'm trusting you to keep this safe for Mosey. It was—"

"His daughter's. Yeah." He didn't want to touch it. He couldn't believe he'd criticized her for saving it, and she *still* wanted him to take it.

"I trust you to get it safely back to Mosey."

It was too much, her looking at him like he'd hung the moon. Unable to refuse, he took it into his hands and debated smashing it into a million pieces because it had almost cost Mallory her life. But he couldn't, not with her sea-green gaze fastened on to him.

After she was tucked into an ambulance, he refused to have his leg checked. It wasn't bleeding, so he'd survive. He always did.

The ambulance rolled away. Shamus started limping in the direction of an officer to see who was lead investigator on the bombing, and that's when he spotted the present Mallory had given him. Its silver ribbons and shiny red wrapping paper were wet from the snow, torn up and blackened some from the blast, but the box was still in one piece.

He picked it up but refused to open it, pretending his knee

didn't hurt, pretending he wasn't angry he didn't stop the bombing somehow...and pretending he wasn't worried about Mallory.

Bowing his head, he thanked God for saving him and Mallory both, and promised that he would not get attached to her, no matter what.

It should be easy enough not to. They had nothing in common. From what he'd observed in the last month, Mallory Larsen always had a kind word about and for everyone. He didn't like to talk at all. She thought she could really help her probationers. He was under no such delusions about his. She was always concerned and wanted everyone to be happy. He had no desire to be happy.

She was sunshine, and he was a thundercloud. Judging by that, when she came to her senses, she wouldn't want a thing to do with him.

And that suited him just fine.

Wondering if she should try calling Shamus again, Mallory nestled into the soft cushions of her best friend's plush white sofa, which was like a balm to her aches and bruises. Ginny had rescued Mallory on Friday night from having to go to her parents' house to recuperate by insisting she'd be more comfortable in Ginny's penthouse. Her mother couldn't even argue with the truth.

Thank goodness.

She watched Ginny gazing out her huge picture window overlooking a major part of Shepherd Falls. Her friend had been pacing for almost an hour and, despite her anxiety over the bombing, still looked every bit like the highly paid fashion model she'd once been, blond hair and makeup perfect. How did she do that?

"Please don't worry, Ginny," Mallory told her. "They're

looking for Tripp, and when they find him, they'll get to the bottom of whoever is behind the bombing."

"I know," Ginny agreed. "But until then, whoever was behind this is out there somewhere, and he might set off more explosions." She moved from the window to her ceiling-high, white-branched Christmas tree to fiddle with the silver-and-blue decorations. "We'll still be in danger."

"But we'll be guarded, since they're moving us to the courthouse, remember?" The basement, anyway, but it was still good. She'd found out about the move when Bess, the chief probation officer, had phoned them to check on her. "We'll have little to nothing to worry about."

Ginny didn't respond, so Mallory went back to the romance novel on her lap. Her mind, however, was on Shamus. Why wasn't he calling back? She'd left three messages on Saturday, and one earlier that afternoon.

She'd call him one final time, she decided. And in this message, she would use gentle persuasion.

"Maybe I ought to hire a bodyguard for you."

Her gaze flew to meet Ginny's. Her friend had more money than she could ever spend from a trust fund and investments made while she'd been a model, but Mallory couldn't let her do that. She did not want to be that far in debt to anyone.

"I don't want a bodyguard. God will watch over me." Even though Ginny wasn't a believer, Mallory reminded her anyway, hoping to be a witness of her faith.

Ginny just stared at her.

"Not only that," Mallory continued, "you've done plenty as it is, letting me stay here so I wouldn't have to go to Mom and Dad's. Mom was sweet in the hospital, but she kept begging me to move back home where I'd be safe. You were a lifesaver. I was close to buckling under the pressure."

"Sure you were." Ginny, who knew better, grinned. She

stepped away from the tree to join Mallory at the other end of the sofa.

"Your dad was there when I arrived to get you. How did it go?"

"He told Mom if I came home I needed to pay room and board."

Ginny winced, her brown eyes filling with sympathy. "You almost got blown up, and that's all your father said?"

Mallory shrugged. After years of that kind of thing out of Gideon Larsen, she'd come to expect it. That didn't mean the words didn't hurt, but there was nothing she could do. No one could change the past, or her part in it.

But it wasn't important now. She had her own life, and her parents had theirs. She picked up her cell from beside her. "It's time for me to try Shamus again. He's going to talk to me whether he wants to or not."

"Since he hasn't answered all your other messages, I'm thinking that's a definite 'not,'" Ginny said, tucking her feet underneath her. "Why on earth would you want to talk to him that badly? He's a jerk."

Mallory held up her hand for Ginny to wait a couple seconds, then answered the other woman's question in the message she left for Shamus.

"Hi, Mallory again. I know you're probably busy trying to help the police find Bud Tripp, and I'm sorry for bothering you so much. It's just, now that I'm well, I have to get started on my promise to help Tara, and I've decided the fastest way to do that would be to find Mr. Tripp myself. I just really wanted to talk to you before I start looking. Thanks."

Mallory tapped the disconnect button triumphantly. "That ought to get a response."

It did. Ginny's feet hit the floor, her long, blond hair swinging. She stood up, her eyes filled with concern.

"Tell me you were going for shock value to get Shamus to call back," she said. "Tell me you're not truly planning on…" Her voice drifted off as her gaze turned horrified at the sight of Mallory's resolute one.

"Oh, Mallory. You *are* going to look for Tripp."

"Of course I am." Mallory put the phone back down beside her. "If I find Mr. Tripp and persuade him to turn himself in, it solves three problems. The police and the FBI will be that much closer to the person behind the bombing and Tara's kidnapping. I won't have to revoke Mr. Tripp's probation, and Tara will have her father home when they find her, not sitting in some jail cell." The teenager would have someone with her who really cared, unlike what had happened to her after…

Ginny shook her head and sat back down. "It's too dangerous for you to get in the middle of this. Whoever is behind the bombing might be just playing games right now while he gets ready to kill someone. Why be a target?"

"If the man *was* a killer, he wouldn't have told Mr. Tripp to get Shamus and me out." She'd had plenty of time to leave before the bomb went off. Getting trapped had been her own fault. "But you agree Tripp couldn't have been behind this?"

"Sure. It's not logical. Why would he want to blow up the building? You said he was basically honest, with a conscience. Plus, you said he was scared to death."

"He was." It felt really good knowing Ginny agreed with her, when the detective in charge had not ruled out Tripp's involvement. Kidnappings, he'd said, had been faked in the past for all sorts of reasons.

"But don't change the subject," Ginny told her. "You might not think Tripp is dangerous, but sometimes you're a little too trusting of people. What if Tripp is ordered to kill you if you try to take him to the police department to be questioned? If the mastermind threatens his daughter's life, who do you think Tripp is going to choose?"

Mallory had to admit she was right about the danger. But she had promised Tara Tripp she would help her, and she couldn't back down. To make Ginny feel better, Mallory compromised. "How about if I just gave my ideas on where to find Tripp to the police?"

Ginny's face filled with relief. "That would be wonderful. And you'll stop talking to Burke, too, right?"

"Uh, no." She wasn't giving in on that. "Why should I stop talking to Shamus?"

"Because he's got to be the one the bomber is targeting, and you could get caught in the middle."

"We don't know Shamus is the target yet." The police weren't telling her a thing.

"Of course we do," Ginny corrected. "You said the man talking to Tripp through the microphone mentioned Burke? I'm betting someone wants to get revenge on him again, the way that man did when he killed Burke's wife.

"Think about it, Mal. In the five years I've been at the probation department, no probationer has attacked us in our building—until Shamus came to work there. Very few people take offense at being monitored by a kind probation officer, but I'll bet a lot did when Mr. Personality was arresting people. He's probably a maniac magnet."

"He hasn't always been like he is now. I told you that when he started working with us." Mallory's face flushed. Keeping calm was an effort, but she was determined to do it. "He was happy. Interested in everyone, and always trying to do things for others."

"I didn't mean to get you upset—you're supposed to be recuperating." Ginny looked genuinely sorry as she picked up a pillow and cradled it in her arms. "I remember when you told me about already knowing him. I never said anything then, but I need to now. You said Shamus was that way at *church*, and you didn't know him otherwise socially. He could have been putting on a front for all of you there to fit in, maybe to please his wife. Who knows? For certain, there have been no signs of the man you're describing in our office. Not one."

Mallory took a deep breath. "I don't think he's a hypocrite, Ginny." Her voice was so calm. God was helping her.

Ginny stared at her for a long moment. "You might want to consider if your heart isn't getting in the way of your common sense where Shamus is concerned."

"I don't have romantic feelings for him." She didn't. Shamus might never change back to the man he once was, and the man he was now was too much like her father. "I was just trying to live my faith and be kind to him."

"Faith." Ginny brushed the idea away with her manicured fingertips. "All month he's ignored you, scowled at you and turned down every offer of friendship, no matter how hurt you looked. What kind of Christian would do that?"

"One who is suffering a great deal of pain," Mallory said firmly.

Ginny put down her pillow and stood. "Sometimes I think you carry Christianity too far, Mal. I don't get how you can let someone walk all over you like Shamus did, and still defend him. I can't. I hope he continues to ignore your calls, because I'd hate it if you got caught right in the middle of his battle with a demon from his past."

Mallory watched her walk down the hall to her kitchen, then stared down at the cell phone by her side. Was she being naïve about Shamus? Was he a hypocrite, putting on a show at church when he was another way at home?

She put that question aside and considered what she knew for certain about him.

He'd saved her life by going back into a burning building for her.

He'd shown true concern for her in his unguarded moments in the parking lot afterward, when he'd held her in his arms.

He'd taken charge of Mosey's Santa so it wouldn't get lost or broken, despite the fact that he was furious she'd gone back for it. For a second she'd thought he would smash it down on the asphalt, but he hadn't.

All that meant Shamus had integrity and feelings—he was just keeping them buried now. Ginny's defenses were up when it came to Shamus for some reason, so she would just keep all of this to herself, along with her plans to find Tripp.

When Ginny returned with a soda and a box of expensive chocolates to share, she didn't mention Shamus or the bombing again, and Mallory was relieved. She loved Ginny like a sister and didn't want anything coming between them. So when her cell phone vibrated in her pocket, she told Ginny she was going to her room for a nap, waited until she got far enough down the hall so Ginny couldn't see and checked the number.

It was Shamus.

THREE

In a moment of insanity, Shamus had agreed to meet Mallory the next day on Holiday Avenue, named on purpose because its shopkeepers had persisted in decorating for every holiday for so many years it had become a tourist attraction in the state. From his table in the rear of the coffee shop where they'd chosen to meet, he had a good view through the windows.

He saw bright lights on Christmas trees in shop windows, a couple of people with charity buckets ringing golden bells and a tall Santa with a thick white beard that looked pretty realistic. He also saw trouble—Mallory, who was parallel-parking her SUV in a space not too far from where he was sitting.

He had hoped his lack of response to her calls would annoy her enough to give up on him, but really, what was he thinking? This was Mallory. For some strange reason, she seemed willing to take all he had to dish out—and cheerfully, too.

When she'd called to say she was going to look for Bud Tripp, Shamus's blood had run cold. Whether Tripp was a victim or the bomber, searching for him would be dangerous. He had to dissuade her from helping Tripp and his daughter, no matter what she'd promised Tara Tripp on the phone.

If Mallory refused to listen, he'd feel obligated to watch out for her, and he wanted no part of that. None. On the other hand, he couldn't take it if something happened to someone else he—no, not liked. Admitting to himself he liked Mallory would create a bond they didn't have. He just didn't want something to happen to someone else he *knew* because of him. Nothing more, nothing less.

He held back a sigh. Why was God doing this to him? Why couldn't He let him just live out the rest of his life paying for not being there for his wife when she died? That's what he wanted. Instead, God had given him—Mallory.

Compared to dealing with her, misery was easy.

Poor Shamus looked absolutely miserable, so Mallory stopped at the sales counter long enough to get some plain coffee for herself and two large sugar cookies with green and red sprinkles, which the clerk bagged along with napkins. The very sight of the decorated cookies made her happy. It didn't get any better than Christmas—and surviving a bomb blast. She would convince Shamus of that, too.

Carrying her snack to his table, she put it down and gave him her most cheerful smile that made most people light up like a Christmas tree.

Shamus's bulbs, apparently, were all burned out.

"Merry Christmas!" she said. "Before I forget again, thank you for saving my life."

"You're welcome," he said. His black-velvet eyes were still guarded, but at least his tone wasn't as frosty as usual. "I take it you're okay?"

"Fine." Bruised and sore, but she was alive, so who cared? "How about you? I heard you were limping after the blast."

"Muscle pull. It worked itself out."

"You're a real hero. Carrying me while you were hurt."

He shrugged. "I was happy to do it, Mallory."

"I hope you still feel that way after we talk."

"Yeah, so do I." He sipped some of his coffee while she slipped out of her jacket and put it on the chair to his right, which she chose so she could have a view of the place. Despite what she'd said to Ginny yesterday about not being afraid, she wasn't stupid. She planned on being careful, just not paranoid.

She needed to forget all Ginny's worries about Shamus. He'd saved her life. His little jab about only doing so for selfish reasons had stung for a few minutes, but he *had* saved her life. That was all that mattered.

Sitting down, she faced him and rubbed the arms of the Victorian red pullover sweater she had knitted herself for warmth, glad she wore it. His silence felt chilly.

She'd just have to be the one to break the ice.

"It's okay if you don't want to be here talking to me, Shamus," she said. "I'm used to it. My probationers are never happy to see me, either."

"I can't imagine why not."

There was a hint of teasing in his voice. Teasing was good. "They're usually not happy because I get information out of them they don't want to give."

"I'll keep that in mind."

"You'll be happy to know I've changed my mind about going after Tripp myself."

He remained silent, his expression guarded, as always.

"Aren't you going to say 'I'm glad' or 'That's good' or something?" she asked.

"I'm waiting for your punch line. You've changed your mind about going after Tripp yourself, but…" He flexed his wrist outward, expecting her to fill in his verbal blank.

"This is me you're talking to. There are no 'buts,' I promise. Ginny convinced me it would be too dangerous to go after him alone."

"So she's going with you?"

"Shamus," she chided gently. "I'm not going to search for him. But I would like an update from you on what's going on with my probationer. All Detective Sullivan said when he questioned me Saturday was that Tripp had escaped the blast after dropping a knapsack in the building, and whether it was the one he was wearing when we saw him or a different one is unknown. Are the police any closer to finding him or his daughter yet?"

Shamus started to say something, but shook his head instead. "What makes you think I would know that?"

"What? You don't?" She twisted her mouth into a smirk. "They do let me supervise lawbreakers, Shamus. I might be cheerful and caring, but I'm not stupid."

He grinned. Full-out and natural. She sucked in a breath at the sudden pull on her heart.

"So there *is* cynicism under all that sweetness," Shamus said.

She shook her head resolutely. "No cynicism in me. I believe in staying positive no matter what. I'm not letting life take away my happiness."

She didn't add "like you did," but she might as well have. His grin disappeared, and his eyes hardened.

"I hope you never have to eat those words, princess. Because I don't think you realize just how bad life can get."

"I'm not a princess," she told him. "I grew up working-class poor with a distant father who started drinking and became emotionally and physically abusive when I was eleven. And—does this sound familiar?—he focused on the bad in life and nothing anyone ever did made him happy to this day, even though he's stopped drinking."

Shamus's eyes narrowed at the sides. Before he had seemed guarded. Now he had that intensity back she'd seen right after the bomb had exploded and she'd opened her eyes while in his arms.

Oh boy, she didn't need to be thinking about that intensity. "What changed your father when you were eleven?" he asked.

"You promise not to think less of me if I tell you?"

His lips parted as if he was surprised by the question, but his gaze never changed. "I don't think there's anything you could say that would change my opinion of you, Mallory."

She didn't want to tell him. Didn't want to think about what had happened that had made her aloof-but-otherwise-okay father into a moody, verbally abusive man who couldn't succeed in drowning his sorrow. But if she told him, maybe he would understand he didn't have to end up being another Gideon Larsen, minus the booze.

It was one way she could pay Shamus back for saving her life.

The story was sad, and she focused on the two children talking to the street Santa outside, hoping the happiness she saw there would get her through it.

She lowered her voice and leaned closer to him so he could hear. "I was eleven, and my older brother was fourteen. My parents both worked, so during the summer vacation, the two of us were responsible for watching our little sister, who was six."

She wanted to stop there, to tell him how pretty and sassy Kelly had been, but if she did, she'd never finish. Just like always when she got to this part in the story, she wanted to cry. Watching the children outside wasn't helping at all, so she transferred her gaze to her coffee cup.

"My brother, Ethan, had a ball game, and he told me to watch Kelly. We walked two blocks to the school playground so she could go on the swings, and then we walked back home and into the house, and I locked the back door. Before our parents got home, I was supposed to put clothes in the dryer and fold a couple of piles of clean laundry in the cellar, but Kelly was afraid of going down there, because sometimes there were mice. So I let her stay upstairs in the kitchen and went downstairs to turn on the dryer. When I finished the work, I went upstairs. The back door was open, and Kelly was gone."

"They didn't find a...her?" he asked quietly.

"No." She met his gaze. His eyes had softened. She had reached him. But there was more. "My father blamed my brother and me both. I didn't think my mother did, but she didn't protect us from his yelling, so maybe subconsciously she did and wanted us to be punished. I don't know. Anyway, Ethan was my best friend after that. Life was rough, and he kept promising me when he was eighteen, he would get an apartment and get me out of there as soon as he could. He said if need be, we'd move to another state."

"It didn't happen?"

"Oh, he got the apartment in another state, I guess. I don't know for certain because he broke all ties with me and didn't leave a forwarding address. Just a note saying he was very, very sorry, but he had to leave. That I would be all right. Haven't heard from him since."

"How long?" Shamus asked, frowning.

"About thirteen years, give or take." She gave him a sad, closed-lipped smile. "It's over and done, all of it. I just wanted to tell you this so you can see I know what misery is. I just choose to follow what the Bible says, that no matter what our circumstances are, we should be content.

"So if I'm happy and try to look at everything in a positive light, Shamus, it's not because I'm stupid or naive. It's because I don't want to lose the life God wants for me."

Like her father had. Like, maybe, Shamus would. She didn't have to say that. Shamus understood. She could tell by the way his features changed to a pensive look.

"You know you weren't responsible for whatever happened to your sister, don't you?" he asked.

"I know it in my head, Shamus. But in here—" she tapped her finger against her chest "—I'm not so sure."

"I know what you mean," he admitted.

He was talking to her about something personal? Her eyes went big, but Shamus shook his head. "That's all I'm saying on that, so don't even try to get me to share."

He was closing off to her again, so she had to get back to the reason why she'd come. "So what's the latest on Tripp?"

"As of this morning," he said, "he's still just a person of interest in the bombing, and his daughter is still missing."

Normally, with Tripp being involved in a felony, Mallory would need to revoke his probation. But in this case, where someone could be holding her probationer hostage by now, and his daughter's life was threatened, it was a gray area, her boss had said. Tripp wasn't supposed to be avoiding the law, but she didn't know for certain that he was.

"Was the backpack they found at the scene the one we saw Tripp wearing, or a different one?"

"I wasn't told," Shamus said.

"But you asked."

One side of his mouth quirked upward, but he didn't reply. That meant he'd asked. Amazing how well she could read him. The very thought of that distracted her for a few seconds while she wondered if it meant anything about him and her. She decided it didn't. She didn't like him well enough for a "him and her" anyway. Her instincts were still sharp, that was all, despite the bomb blast knocking her silly.

"When was his daughter last seen?" she continued.

"Getting off her school bus at three-thirty Friday at the end of her street, by a neighbor. The man blackmailing Tripp—if there is such a man—may have been waiting for her at her house." Shamus glanced at his watch and looked up at her with his eyebrow raised. "Any more questions?"

"Yep." Sliding her chair away from him enough to give herself some elbow room, she opened her bag and took out the two cookies inside. "Want Santa or the reindeer?"

She expected him to be above the obvious bribe to keep him at their meeting, but he grabbed Santa right out of her fingertips. She hid her smile. "You have a weak spot for sweets."

He stopped munching on the cookie abruptly, and swallowed, staring at her. "I guess you could say that."

All of a sudden she felt like a warm sugar cookie.

"And you have brothers," she added quickly to get her mind on where it should be—trying to figure out how best to pay him back. Because baring her soul earlier to make him see he needed to change wasn't enough, she supposed. "Brothers, or a lot of friends."

"Three brothers." He bit Santa's head off. That didn't surprise her at all. "How did you know?" he asked a minute later.

"The way you grabbed Santa. Cookie survival. Before everything went south at home, my brother's friends would come over at Christmas time, and if you weren't fast when cookies came out of the oven, you were out of luck."

A wave of emotion over the loss of her sister and her brother's broken promises threatened her happiness for a few seconds until she shoved back the hurt. Grieving forever wouldn't help a thing—her father had shown her that. She couldn't bring Kelly back and win her father's love or relieve her father's grief. This was all God's plan. Her only responsibility was to look to God and have joy in her heart, not misery.

She pulled out the reindeer with the green sprinkles, broke off a piece and ate, enjoying the taste of the butter and sugar flavors blended together and feeling her tense shoulders relax.

The pure delight in Mallory's eyes teased Shamus's weary heart, and he tried not to let himself warm to her. She'd lived through tragedy and hurt, and kept going. He admired that.

Watching her happy was almost better than eating the cookie she'd bought for him. Definitely better than sitting in his house alone, waiting for the makeshift probation office to re-open tomorrow morning. Infinitely better than waiting for Christmas to pass so he could forget how bleak he felt inside.

He wished he knew how she did the happiness thing. It couldn't only be God, because he'd turned to God over and over and gotten only silence, not joy.

Mallory polished off her cookie, wiped her fingertips and leaned over way too close to him again. He almost bolted away. He could handle Mallory being close. He *could*. He was just edgy because someone had tried to blow him up.

"Any more questions?" he asked her.

"Sure. Lots," she said brightly. "Why do you suppose someone would force Tripp to bring a bomb into the proba-tion building?"

"If you use someone else to do your dirty work, the police have a harder time finding you. The only problem is if the guy talks."

"So you kidnap his daughter to keep him quiet," she said softly. "But how long can that work?"

"Not long. A hostage is a lot of trouble. So is blackmail. Something usually gives in both cases." Shamus's focused stare told Mallory that Tripp and his daughter could already be dead. She worked her teeth along her lower lip. That would be horrible.

She had promised Tara she would help her.

"Why pick Tripp to do the dirty work?" she asked.

"Don't know. I'm sure the police and the FBI are looking into Tripp's associates," Shamus told her. "Maybe it will turn out this isn't about me at all." He didn't believe that, but hope-fully she would and stop asking questions.

As she shook her head back and forth, doubt in her eyes,

Shamus caught an odor of apples and spice, the scent of Christmas. Maybe from her hair. Maybe her cologne.

Maybe he was losing his focus. The cheerful, sweet woman next to him was cutting into his misery like the sugar into the butter used for the cookie he'd just eaten. When she'd been telling her story, he'd almost pulled her into his arms.

He had to get away from Mallory Larsen. He had to forget that she'd awakened an emotion in him that he thought he'd buried—anger. Anger at the sick creep who had abducted her sister, and anger that Mallory had been partially blamed by her father for something she had no control over. He didn't want to feel anger again. It had almost destroyed him while he'd searched for his wife's killer.

He'd rather feel nothing at all.

"We done?" he asked abruptly.

"Not yet, Shamus." She flipped a few long chestnut locks over her shoulder, which drew his gaze to her hair. It was swept upward at both sides with red velvet barrettes, the old-fashioned, Victorian Christmas red his mother was fond of and which matched Mallory's sweater. Miniature green ribbons hung from the ends of the barrettes and cascaded through the silky strands.

He watched her lips move, but he didn't hear a word she said.

"Shamus?" She tapped his arm, and he almost jumped. "So you don't think I'm a target?"

Did he? According to the detective handling the case, there was a lot the police didn't know for certain yet. Probably wouldn't know until they found Bud Tripp or his daughter. But if Shamus told her that, she would worry. He didn't want that on his conscience.

"For now, I'm assuming you weren't the target. The bomber was willing to let you leave. He mentioned my name, but not yours. And besides, you couldn't make an enemy if you tried." All of which were true.

The corners of her mouth lifted briefly. "I need to know for certain. I have to reassure my mother I'm not walking around with a big 'Kill Me' sign on my back. Otherwise, she'll worry to the point of exhaustion."

He shot her a concerned look. "Maybe she needs to take something for that."

"Not her exhaustion. Mine." She pointed her thumb at herself. "I need to reassure her before she worries me to death."

She looked so serious, he didn't smile at her joke. That was Mallory, always worried about someone else, never about herself. But now he understood why. She needed to take care of everyone because she felt she'd failed at watching over her sister.

"All right," he grudgingly said. "The police don't think anyone's after you. But that's all I'm telling you."

She looked like she'd won the lottery. "If Tripp wasn't after me, there *has* to be someone else involved. Because why would Tripp try to blow *you* up on his own? You weren't in on his arrest, were you?"

For her safety, he needed to get her off this fixation she had with the case. "Look, any target in this bombing would more likely be me, not you. Logic says there's more than one person running around loose who'd like to see me dead. So tell your mother you're going back to a secure office in a heavily guarded courthouse basement tomorrow morning, and you'll be fine. That'll take care of her worries."

"Okay." She nodded. "One more question—"

He held up his hand. He'd had enough. Enough of the way her hair flowed over her shoulder whenever she moved her head, enough of her apples and spice, enough of the way she could get him to talk and relax his guard.

"Too many people here. Save the rest of your questions for the detective in charge of the case, okay?" Shamus wasn't just making an excuse. The coffee shop *had* filled up fast with

Christmas shoppers and teenagers out on Christmas break. He didn't want anyone accidentally or purposely hearing what they were saying.

Standing, he slipped on his jacket, picked up his paper cup and walked a couple of feet over to the nearby trash receptacle to toss it in.

When he turned toward the door, Mallory was in front of him with her waves cascading over the fur collar on her jacket, making him want to reach out and touch the beckoning softness. But he couldn't. He didn't want to get involved with her that way. She might make him forget that happiness never stuck around for too long.

"I had one more comment," she said softly, her green eyes begging him to hear her out. He couldn't move. "I need to tell you some things about Tripp's background so you can get proactive about finding him."

He glanced around them—no one seemed to be paying attention. He'd give her one more minute of conversation. "Who said I'm going after anyone?"

"You're not?"

"At this point, I'm letting the police do their own work." That was true. He'd lost his heart for detective work over the agonizing months he'd spent searching for Ruth's murderer and making sure he went to prison. He'd been forced to keep away from his brothers, their families and his mother, partly to make the killer think he didn't care about them so he would leave them alone, and partly because Shamus didn't want his own anger to touch his family. The same hour the man who'd murdered his wife had been sentenced, he'd quit the force and become numb. He wouldn't go after anyone else unless he absolutely had to.

Mallory stared up at him. "You have to search for the bomber. You can't let him just try over and over again to hurt you."

"Excuse me," a patron said, wanting to throw away her

trash. Shamus took Mallory's elbow and moved her back to their table, which still held her coffee and paper bag.

"Remember how you said you owed me for saving your life? I have a couple of ways you can pay me back."

She gave him a short, expectant nod, her eyebrows raised in question.

"Leave all the investigating to the police. Do not get involved in any part of it and make yourself a target. And that includes speculating on Tripp with other people. And don't invite me to join the other probation officers at lunches and after work anymore. I don't want any friends, Mallory."

Her dejected look made him feel as though he'd crushed a rose under his heel. His heart thumped painfully. He had to be this way. He *had* to. Trying to be friends with him would only darken the light Mallory had in her eyes every day. He couldn't take that. He couldn't allow her to become him.

He could hardly stand what he had just done.

"You are such a hard man to like," Mallory told him. "But I'm not giving up on you. You saved my life."

His cell phone played a familiar tune, but Mallory was still standing there, keeping his attention. How could she be so warm and sweet and caring, and still be the most obstinate woman he'd ever run across?

The tune kept playing. He had to answer it. "Excuse me a second," he said, whipping it out and pressing On.

"Hi, Mom. How are you?"

As Mallory watched, the tension drained from Shamus's shoulders and face, and he looked like he used to when he and his wife and she had all sung in the annual Christmas cantata at the homes for the elderly. Relaxed. Happy.

Her mouth dropped open. What Shamus wanted her to do to repay him—stay out of his life—wasn't really going to help him. But she'd just gotten an idea of what might.

She just wasn't certain it would work.

Shamus started scowling as he continued to listen to his mother, and Mallory stayed put, eavesdropping unashamedly.

"No, Mom, don't open the door to him. No one is supposed to be doing an article on me. I'll be right there. What does he look like?"

He muttered "Uh-huh" a couple of times, and then his eyes, filled with alarm, shot up and locked on her. He moved the phone backward and mouthed, "Tripp."

Tripp was at Mrs. Burke's house? Why?

Bringing the phone back to his ear, Shamus gestured for Mallory to follow him. Leaving her coffee behind, she did, darting around a small group of people chatting in the aisle and listening to what he was telling his mother. It was easy enough with his commanding voice.

"Does he have a knapsack or any kind of parcel in his hands? No? Okay. Put as many walls between you and the front door as possible. Do not go outside. I'm only a few blocks away."

On the sidewalk, Shamus broke into a run toward his non-descript sedan. Mallory followed just as quickly and slid into the passenger seat, her heart pounding. Why, oh why, would Tripp bother Shamus's mother? Surely not to hurt her. Not another bomb. Shamus had lost his wife—he couldn't lose another family member.

She didn't think he could take it.

FOUR

Mallory spent the next few minutes getting Shamus's handcuffs out of his glove compartment, calling 911 and remembering to brace herself whenever Shamus rounded corners, tires squealing. His eyes were set on deadly to mess with, and she wouldn't want to be in Tripp's position right now for anything in the world.

"If this is Tripp, he's violating his probation for not reporting in after being involved in a major crime. I should call the boss."

"No time. We're here."

She braced, and Shamus made a turn onto a driveway that led up a hill to a lovely, three-story home. An older, foreign-model car that obviously didn't belong with the house was parked to one side at the bottom of the drive, and Mallory scanned the yard for Tripp.

"He's in the bushes by the front door," she said. As soon as Shamus screeched to a stop near the right side of the house, Mallory swung out of the passenger seat onto her feet.

"Mr. Tripp!" she called over the top of the car to her probationer. "Don't move!"

Rounding the car and heading toward him, she noted that Tripp wore the same thin, close-fitting jacket he'd had on the last time they'd seen him, with no backpack, and no other obvious signs of a bomb.

Thank you for that, Lord.

Tripp bolted down the snow-covered lawn toward his car. She ran after him. Shamus easily passed her to tackle the other man. Snow packed beneath their body weight as the two of them rolled, but Shamus's size and strength stopped Tripp from putting up a fight. Good thing, too, judging from the fury on Shamus's face.

Shamus maneuvered himself upward, leaving one knee in Tripp's back, and yanked on Tripp's shoulders. "Did you plant a bomb here? Did you?"

Worried, Mallory's gaze flew to the front of the house, checking every foot, then back to Tripp.

"You'd better tell him," she warned. "If a bomb goes off, I can't be responsible for what he does to you."

Tripp shook his head furiously, fear pulsating from him. "I swear I didn't plant a bomb," he said, looking more miserable than he had the day of the bombing, if that were possible. "I wouldn't have hidden in the bushes if I had. I have to stay alive to get my daughter back."

Mallory believed him. She also understood the desperation he felt. She would have done anything to rescue her sister, if she'd just had the chance. But that didn't mean she was going to put up with him ignoring the conditions of his probation.

Watching Shamus let Tripp fall back into the snow as he cuffed him, she moved around to kneel in front of them.

"Congratulations, Mr. Tripp. It takes a lot to irritate me, but you've officially done it."

"I'm impressed," Shamus told him. "I've been trying to irritate her for almost a month, and it still hasn't worked."

"You're losing focus," Mallory said, lifting her head to look up at him.

He winked, just to keep her off balance, and then patted their captive down for weapons. Nothing. Shamus gave their surroundings another glance. No backpacks that he could see. He jerked Tripp up by the back of his collar. "So why are you here?"

"I was ordered to come! My daughter's kidnapper—he told me to pretend I was a reporter, to try to get information about you. That was all I was supposed to do."

"How do you get in contact with him?" Shamus asked.

"I can't tell you. He says he'll kill me if I talk to anyone."

Mallory pursed her lips. Tripp had just admitted he was holding back information about who was using him to threaten Shamus. She needed to get it out of him.

"What about your daughter, Mr. Tripp?" she asked. "Don't you want to tell us what you know so we can save her?"

"I came here and did what the man said. He's going to let her go. He promised."

"You're either incredibly naive or unfortunately stupid," Shamus told him, rising and hauling Tripp to his feet.

As much as Tripp was irritating her, Mallory thought as she also got to her feet, she understood him. Tripp was merely hoping for the best. She understood hope, even if Shamus didn't. For two days, she had hoped Kelly was merely lost somewhere and would come back home. There was hope— but there was also reality. Some people didn't come back home, and right now, Tripp didn't have the luxury of remaining silent, not when a life was at stake.

"You can't count on the word of a kidnapper, Mr. Tripp," she said, keeping her tone firm.

Her probationer's face melted like a chocolate Santa held too long in a child's hand. "I talked to Tara before I came here. She even said he promised to let her go if I just did what he asked."

Mallory's irritation grew. She wasn't getting through to him.

She had to. "Stop living in your fantasy world and tell me who has her, *now*," she said, her voice intentionally sharp. She tried to rein in her anger, but couldn't. "If you don't do something, the kidnapper could kill her. You're a father. Act like one."

She caught sight of Shamus's eyebrows rising in surprise, but she ignored him, focusing her gaze on Tripp.

Tripp shook his head miserably. "If I do and he finds out, he *will* kill her. And then he'll kill me."

"Fine." She was done babying Tripp. "This other guy you're so frightened of can kill you, but I can revoke your probation and spread the word in jail you didn't give a hoot about your daughter's life. Take your chances. Who are you more afraid of?"

She walked away, prepared to go immediately to her boss and put everything in motion to put Tripp back in jail. Taking deep breaths, she tried to calm down, but her heart squeezed in fear for Tara. Children should be protected, whether six or sixteen. Tripp needed to be scared. She'd done the right thing.

She hated this job right now.

"Wait!" Tripp called from behind her. She returned to where the two men stood, her back stiffened.

The words poured out of Tripp. "Friday, the kidnapper called me at my new job using my daughter's cell phone. Didn't give a name. He had Tara, and if I wanted her back, all I had to do was get the knapsack, gun and hat he left on my back porch, and pretend I was going to bomb the probation department building. I was to leave the knapsack, which was full of papers. I checked. I was supposed to just scare Mr. Burke. If I did that, he would let Tara go."

Tripp shifted his gaze back and forth over the snow. "But he lied. He must have left another knapsack somewhere in the building and set it off."

Mallory turned to Shamus. His black eyes communicated he wasn't buying one word of it. Her? She wasn't sure what to think.

They could hear sirens in the distance, and Tripp's eyes widened as he looked at Mallory. "Are you going to revoke my probation? Who will take care of my daughter?"

"I'm not certain about the revocation yet." She was inclined to believe Tripp, but she'd have to see what happened with the police first. "The detectives and the FBI will need to question you, so you'll have to go downtown."

Tripp's lips tightened together and his eyes squinted. "My cell phone is in my car on the seat," he said suddenly. "Please get it, Ms. Larsen. I don't know if the kidnapper will let Tara go for sure, but if she gets free, she'll try to call me, not the police. If I'm in jail I can't help her, but you can."

"Why wouldn't she call the police?" Shamus asked.

"She just won't," Tripp said. "I know her."

"I'll help her. I promised." Mallory turned and headed to Tripp's car, purposely not looking at Shamus because he'd say the phone was evidence. Do not touch. But it was also the only number Tara Tripp knew to call, her lifeline to her father, and she needed it more than the police.

She found the phone and stashed it in her deep jacket pocket. Seconds later she headed back toward the two men and was about five feet away, when she heard a loud noise crack through the air.

She whipped around, saw nothing. Wondered if it was a car backfiring. Turned back, saw Tripp folded over in the snow, blood soaking through his jacket in the back.

Her mouth opened, and she breathed shallow, short breaths, unable to move. She didn't understand why. She was in danger of being shot next. Tripp was in danger of being shot again. She should help him get to safety.

But the kidnapper was here....

Shamus grabbed her wrist and pulled her toward his vehicle. "We've got to help Tripp," she breathed out.

"Do you want to get shot, too?" he growled, pulling hard on her arm. "C'mon!"

Still Mallory hesitated, trying to get to Tripp. Then another shot split the air, so close she could feel it. Gathering her wits, she ran with Shamus for cover. Snow crunched under their feet, and she almost slipped, but Shamus's strong arm went around her waist and caught her. They ducked in front of his sedan just as the police siren got louder. They'd warn the gunman off. No, wait—she'd heard the sirens before he'd shot Tripp.

The bomber wasn't afraid of being caught.

As Shamus pulled his Glock and his cell phone out, she sucked in the cold air right down to the bottom of her lungs, praying for God to stop her fear. In four days, she could have died twice. The first time by being in denial that something terrible like a bombing could happen in the peaceful world she'd created for herself, and the second time by letting fear overcome her. She had to get a grip.

The trouble was, she didn't want to have to. She wanted her serene life back.

She could hear Shamus talking to someone, reporting the shot fired and asking for an ambulance, and then he was off his cell phone and picking up his gun from the ground right by them.

"The police should be here any second. You watch behind us. I'll watch in front." He waited until she had changed position and added, "Are you all right?"

She glanced at him. "Of course I'm all right," she said softly. "There were only two shots fired, and we know where they went. What makes you think I'm not all right?"

"You stopped talking. I figured you must be near death."

She blinked. He wasn't grinning, and no twinkle lit his eyes. "You made a joke."

"I did not."

"Yes, you did. It must be the shock from the explosion finally setting in."

"Couldn't be. I'm too busy saving your life to go into shock."

"You did," she said, finding it once again hard to breathe, staring into his eyes. She'd just stood there watching Tripp bleed, and Shamus had pulled her to safety. If he hadn't, she could have been the next victim. "You saved my life again. Now I *really* owe you."

"All I want from you is an explanation of why you went off on your probationer back there." Shamus waved his thumb toward where Tripp still lay. "You were so furious at Tripp, for a few seconds I thought the shot came from you."

"From me?" Incredulous, she mock-slapped his arm to shame him. Or maybe she meant the slap. She wasn't sure. "Me, shoot someone in anger? That isn't funny." She paused. "No, wait, you don't do humor."

"And I've never seen you do furious," he countered. "So what gave back there?"

"Tripp wasn't putting his daughter first. It's the only thing that can push my buttons."

Shamus's eyes were dark pools of sympathy mixed with pain. "Anger can't bring her back, Mallory."

The reminder of her helplessness in that regard brought a lump to her throat that hurt and made her eyes hot. Of course Shamus could relate exactly to what she was feeling. He must have survived his wife's death emotionally by being angry. And even though her killer had been brought to justice, he was still angry. It showed every day at work.

"You're right," she admitted. "And I hate getting angry like that. I'll work on changing."

His deep-throated chuckle warmed her. "Princess," he said in a way that made her forget all about the danger they were in, "I wouldn't want anything about you to change."

Strange butterfly feelings fluttered around her heart that she'd never felt before and did not want to feel now. Not with this guy. Shamus was not dating material, and she didn't want that kind of closeness to the man.

"Why do you keep calling me princess?" she asked, mostly to make herself irritated that he persisted in doing so even when she'd told him she wasn't one.

"To remind me you're untouchable."

That would imply he was thinking… He was thinking what she'd been thinking, and that was simply unthinkable.

"Okay," she said, dragging out the word, swiveling away from him and surveying the front street, keeping as low as she could. "Tripp could be dying. Where on earth are the police?"

More importantly, Shamus thought, how had she gotten him to just say what he was thinking like that? Now he knew how her probationers had to feel. Talking to her *was* dangerous, and he needed to pull back from her captivating personality before he got sucked in by it. Mallory Larsen was not his future. He had no future, just a past of neglecting the last woman he had loved—a past that he couldn't overcome. No way he needed to drag Mallory into that.

"Your poor mother must be scared to death," Mallory said, then tapped her forehead with her fingers. "Sorry. Wrong choice of words." She changed direction again. Behind her, all she spotted were expensive homes and pristine, snow-covered shrubs. There was no one out there.

"The police are here," Shamus told her, rising as he holstered his Glock. "It's safe to get up. The bomber could have picked either of us off already. I think he left as soon as he got the target he wanted."

Mallory stood too, crossing her arms at her chest to rub her forearms, chilled despite the warmth of her jacket. "I'm going to see if I can help Tripp."

He caught her arm to stop her. "One of our officers is with him."

She glanced over her shoulder, saw Shamus was right and then pursed her lips. "I hope he's not dead."

"So do I. If he's dead, we'll never know what else he had to tell us about the kidnapper."

"You're cold."

"Yeah. Warm and fuzzy worrying about your probationers during a sniper attack gets you killed in this world. Keep it in mind for the future."

"I was like you for a long time after...all that stuff happened, you know." She watched an officer in the police cruiser make a turn in front of them, then back up until he was horizontal to Shamus's sedan, providing a shield. "All cynical."

"You're not cynical anymore," Shamus said. "What happened?"

"I got sick of myself."

"Then what?"

"I made the choice to be happy."

"Just like that?"

She nodded her head.

"Well, I ain't you, princess."

She wanted to tell him he could be, that joy was a choice and found in their Savior, but then a car door shut and they heard the voice of a dispatcher on a nearby police radio. Sharing time was over.

"We're behind the car," Shamus called out to the responding officers.

"You okay, Burke?" one of them called back.

Shamus recognized him. James Henley had occasionally helped him while he'd taken down his wife's killer. "I'm fine, but the shooter could still be out there."

"We've got people searching the area. That's what took us so long. My partner's seeing about Tripp." Henley watched both him and Mallory with eyes that were deceptively calm. Shamus knew Henley was a "by the book" type of cop, so he pulled his gun out and handed it to him without the other man having to ask him to.

"When did the shooting happen?" Henley asked as he checked the weapon.

Shamus glanced at his watch. "About five minutes ago."

Henley's gaze swung over to Mallory, who nodded in affirmation, and then he handed Shamus's firearm back to him. "You're clear," he said, taking his notebook out to jot down a few words.

"Good. My mother's alone in the house. I need to make sure she's okay."

"After you do that, we'll want to question you both," the officer replied.

Mallory saw the hesitancy in Shamus's eyes as he turned his gaze to her. "Coming with me?"

She shook her head. A time-out from Shamus, she figured, would be very good right then. "I want to check on something."

"Tripp." Shamus just shook his head, turned and headed toward the back of the house, where she assumed there was an entrance. She hurried down the hill to talk to Tripp, assuming he could still speak. She introduced herself to the officer, showed her identification and was given permission to talk to him.

"Better hurry, though—he's not doing well. Paramedics should be here shortly."

She nodded and knelt down next to Tripp, who was now lying out flat in the snow, a blanket under his head. "Mr. Tripp…"

Tripp's eyes opened, and his hand went up to grip hers. His fingers were icy against her pocket-warmed ones. Icy like death. "School. At her...school," he said, then closed his eyes again.

"What's at Tara's school?" He wasn't making sense. The only thing she could think of was he wanted her to talk to Tara's friends, so she would do that. But he seemed totally out of it now, so more questioning would have to wait till he recovered a bit.

"I'll come to the hospital to see you later," she said, patting his hand. "We'll talk when you're better."

His grip tightened. "Promise me, you'll find her, help her." The words rushed out. "Promise!"

A sheen of sweat broke out on her forehead. *Lord, don't ask this of me.*

What if she couldn't find Tara, like she hadn't been able to find Kelly? Surely God didn't expect her to promise a man who could be dying something that she might not be able to do.

"Please!"

He looked so desperate. What if he died? Who would Tara have then? No one except an overworked police department. She pulled in the deepest breath she could ever remember taking.

"I promise."

He went limp, his eyes shutting. The officer checked him quickly, and nodded at her. "He's still alive."

Asking him to call her if that changed, she handed him one of her business cards and went to find Shamus. He was just inside the kitchen door, taking off his boots.

"House rule when it snows," Shamus said, not looking at her.

"No prob. Unless, of course, something else happens and we have to run outside into the snow quickly, but honestly, who would be worried about that? Not I."

Shamus finally graced her with his attention, one eyebrow raised at her. "If something happens, I'll carry you."

He probably meant in the snow, as opposed to "get you through it." She gave him a tiny smile, her mind still on her promise to Tripp. "Thanks."

"Don't mention it. I'm getting used to it."

So was she. And that could very well be a problem.

Leaning down, she undid her own laces and slipped off one of her sneaker boots. "Tripp's still alive," she told him. "But just barely."

"I hope he pulls through. I want another crack at him."

"If he dies, Shamus," she said, keeping her voice even, trying to suppress her own sadness on Tara's behalf, "think of how his daughter is going to feel."

"He was coming after my mother. Pardon me if I don't have any sympathy." Shamus rose and started through the kitchen, toward a doorway, where he stopped and called out, "Mom, it's safe. Come on out."

Mallory put her foot down, no longer wanting to stay inside. She'd thought she was getting through to Shamus at times, but no. He couldn't even dredge up *some* sympathy for a kidnapped teenager? He was reminding her of her father again, and his cold cynicism was going right to her heart. She wasn't angry, but it hurt.

She sat there, wanting to pull her shoe back on and then call a cab to get back to her SUV, but instead, she debated with God.

Or more like wrestled.

God would not want her to give up on Shamus. Ginny had been wrong about him. His true character had surfaced earlier, in little bits and pieces, and it wasn't harsh and uncaring. He just reverted back to being that way to get him through the pain he was in. But every time he did, he hurt her. No matter how much she wanted to repay him kindness for kindness, just to help him have a life again, she was no martyr.

On the other hand, if she left now, she lost a chance to talk to Shamus's mother and find out if her earlier thought on how to repay him for saving her life might work. But that would mean putting up with Shamus's attitude. Unless she got angry with him, and she didn't want to do that, either.

Lifting her foot up, she made her decision.

FIVE

She couldn't leave. Mothers talked about their sons, and she needed to be here to see if anything Mrs. Burke said might help her figure out a definite way to pay Shamus back. She didn't like owing anyone. Her father had borrowed money he didn't have hiring people to find Kelly and hadn't been able to pay it back. They'd gotten even poorer, and she'd been the object of pity at school and church. At home she'd heard constantly about the shame her father felt about being in debt. She'd sworn she'd never be indebted to a soul.

She especially didn't want to be indebted to Shamus.

Sighing, she took off her second shoe and hurried through the huge kitchen to catch up to him. It was filled with shiny appliances in silver, with snowmen canisters on one counter and shiny red-and-green ornament magnets on the refrigerator.

She and Mrs. Burke were going to get along fine.

"The kitchen's huge," she said when she caught up to him. "Looks like your mother does a lot of entertaining."

"She does. The three brothers I told you about? They're all married."

Just as Shamus used to be. His voice was edged with sadness. Maybe she could repay him by matchmaking. She would have to advertise in the paper, since her own female friends would flee the second she suggested such an idea to them. All three had met Shamus. They wouldn't date him for money. Not even big money.

"Shamus!" a woman called from down the hall. "Did I hear you right? It's okay to come out?"

"The police are here."

"Well, thank goodness." A petite woman emerged from a doorway. She was somewhere in her fifties, with Shamus's black hair, only tinged with gray, and his dark eyes, only hers were warm as she looked at her son and then at Mallory.

"Mallory! I saw your picture in the paper. You're even more beautiful in person."

Mallory's cheeks heated, but she had to smile just looking at the woman. Shamus's mother radiated happiness the same way Shamus did gloom.

"I'm happy to see you're okay, Mrs. Burke. We were really worried about you."

"Thank you. You can call me Susan." She turned back to her son. "She's every bit as nice as you said."

Mallory was shocked Shamus had actually said that to his mother about her. She would have imagined he would say something more like "She's quite a pest."

"You really think I'm nice?" she asked him.

"Actually, nice isn't the word I'm thinking right now." Shamus said. "Mom, no matchmaking. The last person Mallory needs in her life is me."

Mallory supposed that was a better reason to give than "she would drive him crazy."

"I'll try to remember," Susan Burke said, waving her hand, "but I'm not making any promises." She pinned her son with her stare. "So why was that man here, if not to write an article about you? And what were all the police sirens about?"

Shamus hesitated. "You aren't going to like this—"

"I am not moving in with your brother again. Not another word until I get some coffee. I need some fortification." Susan twirled around and headed down the hallway to the kitchen.

Mallory caught Shamus's arm. She didn't want to be caught in a family argument. Not even if she did need to talk to Susan Burke about Shamus. "Should I go outside?"

"Stay. She likes you. It might help."

How could she turn down his direct invitation? She followed him back to the kitchen, arriving just as his mother finished pouring herself a cup of coffee.

"Help yourselves, then you can start telling me what I probably don't want to hear," she said, taking her coffee to a table in front of long windows that gave a view of tall brown trees and green pines in woods covered with a white sheet of snow. The peace Mallory saw outside that window was totally separate from the shooting scene in the front yard.

Mallory got a cup of coffee and joined her. Shamus sat down, too—without coffee. It took him a few minutes to fill his mother in and not answer most of her questions. Mallory felt sure that he wouldn't lie to his mother, so she assumed he really didn't know the answers. He hadn't just been holding back with her.

That made her happy.

"So you can see I'm not just being paranoid here, Mom. The bomber knows where you live—he just tried to use you to get to me. You'll be safer with Rory and his wife."

Rory had to be one of his brothers.

Susan shook her head. "I'm not going anywhere. If the bomber had wanted to hurt me, he could have anytime this morning. I've been in and out twice on various errands. I think he was more than likely wanting to off his witness to keep him from talking."

Mallory's mouth dropped open. Susan gave her a beatific smile. "Don't be surprised, Mallory. Where do you think he got his detective skills from?"

"Mom—"

"I have a better idea," Susan broke in gently. "If you're that worried, how about if you just move here until this guy is caught?"

Shamus's face said that was the last thing he was expecting her to say. He looked from his mother to Mallory.

"It's an idea, Shamus."

"No."

"Well, now you see what I'm saying," Susan said. "I don't want to disrupt my life again, either. I'll be fine, don't worry. Now for the important stuff. Are you coming for Christmas dinner? The whole family will be here."

Shamus looked like a kicked puppy at the very thought. Mallory felt bad for him all over again.

"I'll let you know," he told Susan. "I might have to work."

Mallory stared at him with her eyebrows high and her chin tilted in chastisement. He didn't have to work on Christmas, or even Christmas Eve. Susan couldn't miss her look, which meant now she'd realize Mallory was a *lot* involved in Shamus's life. Shamus was going to really love that.

Shamus met her censuring gaze directly. "Did you ever consider that one of the best days to revoke clients' probation is on a holiday? They won't be expecting me."

"You are in need of some serious help," she told him.

One of his dark looks was her reward for pushing him toward a family Christmas. She just tilted her chin right back at him.

He gave in first. "Please excuse me for a minute or two, Mom. I have to check on a couple things outside."

He headed toward the back door, and, Mallory presumed,

his shoes. Sipping her coffee, Susan waited until she heard the back door close, and then she spoke.

"He's changed so much since Ruth's murder. He blames himself, you know."

That's what had made him the way he was? She had assumed it was grief. Anger at God maybe. But guilt?

"No, I hadn't realized that." She wanted to ask Susan for details, but she thought that might imply an interest in her son Mallory didn't have.

Much.

"I did know something had changed since we participated in the Christmas cantata a couple years back," Mallory added, "but I didn't know why."

"He told me about knowing you slightly from the cantatas." Susan sighed wistfully. "I sure wish he would go back to church. He loved to sing so much. And he really enjoyed going to the rest homes. He even made friends with one older gentleman and used to go back to play chess."

"I hadn't known that." Church. Loved to sing. Played chess with an elderly resident. Mallory's eyes narrowed. They were pieces of her puzzle of how to pay back Shamus by helping him, but she wasn't certain how they fit together yet. "Do you remember the man's name?"

Susan's brow furrowed, and finally she gave up. "I'm sorry, it's been a while. Why?"

Mallory dismissed the question with a wave of her fingers. She didn't want to tell his mother her plan for repaying Shamus when she wasn't even certain what it was yet. "I was wondering if I knew him."

"Oh. Just ask Shamus, dear. I'm sure he'll tell you." Her black-velvet eyes met Mallory's. "Shamus has a wonderful bass voice. I sure miss hearing him sing. And I sure miss having him like he was."

Susan Burke must have been a wonderful mother when Shamus was growing up. She sounded so sad that Mallory wanted to do something to reassure her, but how could she?

"I'm not certain what I can do," she told the older woman.

"Just pray for him. That's what I'm doing. Praying that the Lord will help him, and soon." As quickly as she'd frowned, Shamus's mother rallied, and her smile came back. "I know God will. After all, it's the season of miracles."

The season of miracles. The hope that had rung out in the other woman's words had kept replaying in Mallory's mind while she waited for Shamus in his car outside the Burke family home. Shamus's mother wanted a miracle for her son, so he would start caring about life again, and Mallory wanted to pay Shamus back, so she could get him out of her life. God must want her to get involved in Shamus's life, no matter how much she didn't want to, because He had given her a solution to how to bring about both.

With God's help, of course.

She watched yet another officer arrive, a portly man in his fifties. That made six now, plus the homicide detective, whom she did not like at all. Dickerson was his name. Hopefully amongst them all, they'd be able to figure out who had shot Tripp. Then she saw Shamus heading toward her, hopefully ready to have his life changed.

He slid into the driver's seat, not even acknowledging she was there. As he started the car and put it into drive, she didn't waste any time.

"What was the name of the elderly gentleman you visited at the rest home?"

Shamus came to a stop at the end of the drive and stared at her with surprised eyes.

"Your mother mentioned it," she explained.

"Why do you want to know?"

"I know some of the residents at the places we sing and was curious." Among other reasons.

He didn't answer, just went back to driving them out of the subdivision and onto a major highway with its strip malls, warehouse shopping centers, and fast-food places. He was being stubborn again.

Lord, if someone was supposed to be Shamus's Christmas miracle, why did it have to be her?

Anyone but me, please, Lord.

How was she going to get through to him?

That's when it came to her. She *had* been getting to him—through kindness—and she had to keep that up. It had failed with her father, but maybe, just maybe, it was the way through to Shamus.

He pulled to a stop at a light near Holiday Avenue, where she'd left her car. She took a deep breath, summoned a smile to her lips, and turned to him.

"But if you don't want to tell me, that's all right. I understand."

For a few seconds, he stared at her, shaking his head back and forth as if perplexed.

"How do you do that?" he asked finally. "How do you always turn the other cheek when someone is being impolite?"

She parted her lips in a smile. "You were being impolite just now? I thought that was just you being normal."

The sudden grin on his mouth relaxed his tense jaw and lit up his eyes. A jolt of gladness ran through her. She didn't know what the jolt meant, but she did know it probably wasn't good news. Best to pretend it had never happened and not be pleased she'd made him happy, however briefly. Beyond repaying her debt to him, she could not get further involved.

"There's just something about you, Mallory," he said, shaking his head once more and stepping on the gas. Since she had him all softened up, it was probably a good time to hit him with her plan.

"Shamus, remember earlier you said I could repay you for saving me by leaving you totally alone at work? We kind of left our discussion in the middle when your mother called."

"Yeah," he said as he turned onto Holiday Avenue. "And?"

"I might agree to giving up on all investigations of whoever is after you," she said carefully, because she had no intention of giving up on finding Tara, "and leave you alone at work to boot, if you'll do one more thing for me."

His mouth twisted into a half grin. "What, saving your life twice wasn't enough?"

She melted. He was awfully hard not to like when he stopped being so stoic.

"Really, it's for your mother, as a Christmas present. Something only you could give her." The last part was just plain inspired, and Mallory thought that was probably because she'd chosen rightly with the request she was about to make. The pieces of the puzzle falling into place and all that. If Shamus said yes, she'd be figuratively saving his life and making Susan Burke happy to boot. A win-win situation. She'd have to make sure he stuck by it, and that would be difficult to juggle while looking for Tara Tripp. But she was going to trust God on this one.

"Go ahead, hit me with it," he said, still sounding amused as he slid into a parking place right outside of Caffeine and Cookies, the coffee shop.

"We have two choir rehearsals left for the Christmas cantata. We'll be performing at two places. You already know most of the songs—it shouldn't be too hard to pick up the rest." She paused and drew a breath. "Join us this year? Go to both rehearsals and at least one performance? Your mother would love knowing you were singing again, especially at Christmas. It could be a special present for her."

Silence. Dead silence. Mallory's heart beat harder as Shamus continued to look at her. Then, abruptly, he sat back in his seat and stared out at the city sidewalk. She had no idea what he was going to decide, but it wasn't looking good.

Shamus kept his mouth clamped closed on purpose. The minute he said no, Mallory was going to argue with him. He was positive about that. If he sat there long enough, maybe she would go away.

"Please say yes," she said.

Who was he kidding? She wasn't going anywhere. But her enthusiastic plea was compelling, and he switched his stare from a nearby lamp pole wrapped up in candy-cane ribbons to her green eyes.

That was a mistake. He found himself wondering what life would be like if he just let her win and get him involved again with people. Not even that. What would his life be like if he just quit resisting her being in it? Would some of the ache in his heart from having failed Ruth go away? Because if there was anyone he might let in, it would be Mallory.

But reality dictated that he couldn't think like that.

"Someone's after me, Mallory. The more you're around me, the bigger the risk he might think we're involved and try to hurt you to get to me."

She looked surprised. "Well, that's silly, Shamus. You're the last person I would become involved with."

"What's wrong with—" he began before he could stop himself. Oh man. She *was* getting to him. "Never mind. I don't want to know."

"Sure." She smiled as though she didn't believe him, and that irritated Shamus.

"Anyway," she continued, "someone thinking we're involved won't be a problem. At the office, we can keep our communication work-related. As for the Christmas program, last year we had around twenty people at every rehearsal, a big enough crowd that we don't even have to talk to each other."

He briefly turned his head and closed his eyes to shut out her image.

"I know," she said, "you're thinking 'If only she *would* stop talking to me.'"

Actually, she was wrong. What he *was* thinking was that Mallory's smile had enough wattage to keep the huge, decorated Christmas tree in the city square across from their church—the one he no longer attended—lit up for a year. Enough electricity to warm up his cold heart—if he let it. And that's why he couldn't look at her.

"Besides," she added, "if someone is watching us, I'll be hanging around this guy at rehearsals that I'm sort of dating."

She was dating? Shamus swallowed hard. What kind of man would she date? Someone like herself, probably. Kind hearted, into helping others, talkative. He didn't even know why he was wondering.

"Who?" he asked, his eyes back on her.

"Who did you play chess with?" she countered.

"Mr. Widemeyer."

"The guy at church? He's just a friend. No big deal." Mallory waved her hand to punctuate that. "The point of it is we won't have to worry about the focus being on us as a couple, assuming we don't arrive together."

What she said made sense. And his mother *would* be extremely pleased to see him put forth some effort this Christmas.

And most important, after it was all done, he could be sure Mallory Larsen would be out of his life, where she'd be safe.

"You'll promise not to bother me at work about socializing, and you won't go after the bomber?"

Mallory worked her bottom lip.

"Mallory?" he said.

"I'm not planning on going after the bomber. But I am planning on finding Tara and helping her. I promised Mr. Tripp I would. I'm just not sure how I'm going to accomplish it yet."

"Leave it alone, Mallory." Even as he said it, he knew she wasn't going to obey him. "Let the police handle the kidnapping."

Mallory caught that. "I thought the FBI was handling it. What happened to them?"

Stop talking around her, Shamus reminded himself. "They pulled out, saying there's no proof there was a kidnapping. But the police are looking for Tara."

"And how hard will they look, if the FBI won't work on it?"

She was correct, and Shamus didn't bother to deny it.

"Your lack of response tells me everything," Mallory said. "I'm going to look for her. Don't worry. If I stumble across the bomber, I'll call you."

Shamus threw his palms upward. "I'm not going to keep saving your life if you're this determined to lose it."

"Yes, you will," she told him, her voice softening. "Because you're like that. You're a hero."

"I'm not," he denied, his voice suddenly harsh. "I'm not even close."

She blinked at him, once again looking wounded. He was hurting her too much, and he couldn't keep having contact with her like this. There was only one way he could think of to fix it.

"All right. If you promise to stay out of the bombing investigation and not bother me at work, then I'll do two rehearsals and one performance. Agreed?"

If he didn't know better, he would have thought she was about to hug him. He shifted quickly backward against his car door, just in case, but she didn't lean forward. Instead, she just nodded at him.

"Our next rehearsal is Wednesday at six. You aren't going to regret this, Shamus."

She was wrong, Shamus thought as she said goodbye and left him feeling entirely alone. He wouldn't have her talking to him at work anymore. He wouldn't have her smiling at him anymore. He wouldn't have her caring about him anymore. Yeah, she was wrong. He already regretted agreeing to her plan.

But to keep her safe from his stalker, who was at least a bomber and a possible killer, and to keep her safe from the misery he himself would bring her, it was the only way.

SIX

Finally back home, Mallory tossed her jacket on the couch, made a pot of apple-and-spice herbal tea and sat down with it. She had some planning to do. Shamus might have agreed to the cantata, but she would need to see that he followed through and actually attended. She would need to pray for guidance, and then there would be a phone call or two to see if Mr. Widemeyer—

Loud, jarring tones rang out next to her, coming from inside her jacket on the couch. Tripp's cell phone. She'd totally forgotten she had it.

Her heart pounding—what if it was the kidnapper?—she yanked it out of her pocket and answered it with a short, unsure "Yes?"

No one spoke for a few seconds, and then a young, feminine voice said, "Who are you? Where's my dad?"

"Tara? It's Mallory Larsen, your father's probation officer. Are you all right? Where are you?" *Let me come help you, please.*

"I'm all right. I escaped. Where's my dad? Why do you have his cell?"

What to tell her? Hearing her father had been shot would undoubtedly frighten Tara even more than she already was, but the teenager needed to know so she could go to the hospital and see him.

Just in case.

"Tara," Mallory said gently, "your dad was shot. Let me pick you up, and I'll take you to Shepherd Falls Memorial to see him."

"No!" she wailed. "He'll kill me, too. I know he will!"

She had to be referring to the bomber. Feeling the teenager's anguish clear to her soul, Mallory took a deep breath. She'd do the young girl no good if she fell apart. "Let me help you. Where are you? I can come—"

"Don't come," Tara wailed. "He was mad when you said Friday you would help me. If he's watching you, he'll follow you back to me. I'm going into hiding so he can't find me."

A chill went down Mallory's spine. The feeling of powerlessness was waiting, ready to overwhelm her, just like when she'd been eleven. She couldn't let it.

"Where are you, Tara?" she asked again, more forcefully this time. No response. Finally, she had to accept that the teenager had hung up.

Her fingers punched on the phone buttons until she found the log of incoming phone calls with the numbers. Scratching the latest entry down on paper, she dialed it.

"Tromboni's Pizza, Fourth Street," a man said.

She hung up, grabbed her keys and purse, and flew out the door to her car, heading toward Tromboni's. When she got close enough, she scanned the brightly lit streets everywhere she could without throwing off her driving, but didn't see Tara anywhere. She went into Tromboni's to ask around, found out there had been a girl with Tara when she'd borrowed the business phone, got a description of both girls, and then drove out to the Tripp house, which was dark and abandoned.

Tara Tripp had disappeared all over again.

* * *

The probation department reopened Tuesday morning in its temporary location, in the basement of the county's courthouse, which boasted armed guards, a metal detector and an alarm system. And there was Shamus Burke working diligently at his desk at the far side of the room.

Plenty of protection—assuming Shamus wasn't furious at her. Last night, when she'd gone to the police station to give them Tripp's phone and to report hearing from Tara so they could set up a watch at the hospital for her, she'd realized that Shamus would probably find out about her going to the Tripps' rented house alone and wouldn't be happy with her. Maybe the police would keep it quiet.

"Mallory!" Mosey Burnham boomed out from his work station, rising to his feet.

Hearing her name, Shamus lifted his head. Gone was the usual impenetrable look. He was scowling. Oh boy. Hopefully, the empty desk next to his wasn't meant for her. Wondering how long she could avoid speaking to him, she made a beeline to Mosey Burnham's desk.

"Santa made it back to you!" She pressed the top of the toy's head and laughed delightedly along with Santa. It was the happiest toy she'd ever seen, and she loved it.

"Santa was the only thing on my desk saved." Mosey grinned, but every minute of his fifty-some years was showing on his face as he hugged her and said, "Very glad to see you made it out alive, sweetheart."

His endearment touched her heart. Her own father hadn't said anything about being glad she was still here—not on Friday at the hospital, or several years ago, when her sister had been kidnapped. And knowing Mosey had lost his own daughter and could still say that meant a lot.

"Thank you," Mosey added, his voice heavy with emotion.

"I know you went back for it. You shouldn't have risked your life. But thank you."

"You're very welcome. Most of the credit goes to Shamus. He got Santa and me both out. He's secretly a great guy."

"I am not," Shamus said from his desk, his fingers never missing a key on his laptop as he shot her a warning look. She'd just broken their agreement about no communication outside business at work. This was going to be much harder than she'd imagined.

"Where do I sit?" she asked Mosey.

"Your salvaged computer is right there." He pointed directly to the desk by Shamus's.

"That—" she cut off the words "is wonderful" and substituted "—will work." Shamus didn't look up this time.

She was learning.

She hung up her beige coat on the rack between the door and Ginny's desk. It nestled against Shamus's black leather jacket and looked cozier than she was going to be, sitting next to him today.

Mosey began filling her in. "Ginny came in earlier and went back out again. Her desk is by the door, and she's already not happy with that. Jessica and Renzo are along the far wall—but neither of them have been in yet to complain. Bess said the seating arrangements are meant to keep the gossiping down."

She hid a smile. And in the middle, she'd put Mosey, the office telephone. Information went in his ears and out his mouth, and you didn't even have to press any buttons to make a connection. "Where is Bess?"

"Court. She'll be back in about an hour."

"Thanks."

She sat in her chair, a castoff from the county salvage,

probably. Eager to review Tripp's file for any information she might not remember that would help her find Tara's hiding place, she typed in her password and called up Tripp's file.

And then heard Shamus rolling his chair over to the side of her desk.

"If you're about to lecture me about searching for Tripp's daughter—please don't," she said before he could get started. She gazed at him, waiting.

"Tripp's dead." He raised his eyebrows as what she said sank in. "You searched for Tara?"

"She called on Tripp's cell. He's dead?" Mallory's heart fell. Poor Tara. She would be devastated. And there was no one to take her in, either.

"He died this morning from the gunshot," Shamus confirmed. "When did she call?"

"Right after I got home yesterday, from Tromboni's Pizza. The detective didn't update you?"

"I'm not in this investigation, remember?" He gave one slow shake of his head. "What did Tara say?"

"You sound like you're in it to me," she told him. "Tara said she'd escaped from the kidnapper. I told her about her father, and she said not to come after her. That if the bomber was watching me, I would lead him right to her, and he would kill her just like her father."

"So you went to find her." He said it like he knew the answer and didn't like it.

"Of course I did. Searched the streets from the pizza joint all the way to her house and even scouted around it. Didn't have any luck, though." She stopped to take a breath. "She's all alone out there, Shamus, with no one to care. I had to look for her. I promised Tripp on his deathbed."

The whole time she was speaking, Shamus had the same impenetrable look he'd had before the bombing, so Mallory had no idea what he was thinking, but she hoped he would offer to help her find Tara.

But all he said was, "Please leave Tara Tripp to the police."

She shook her head in refusal. "I'm sorry, I can't just sit here and work and pretend she's not out there alone and vulnerable. I won't."

He finally blinked, and the hard line of his jaw softened. "Look, I understand why you're doing this. All I can do is point out that even Tara told you getting into the middle of this case is too risky. What if the kidnapper is looking for Tara and gets the two of you? I would have to come rescue you again. It's too dangerous, and frankly, I have work to do."

With two pushes of his legs he returned to his desk and started typing, and she sat there watching him and grinning. He just admitted he would come if she needed him.

She pushed her own chair over to his desk, only half taking in that Mosey was watching them both with astonished eyes and that the older probation officer had no doubt heard everything she uttered from her big mouth.

"You would, Shamus? Come rescue me again? Even though I annoy the tar out of you?"

Uttering what sounded like a groan of pain, he swung his gaze from his computer screen to her. "Keep pushing, and I'll have to think about it first."

"You're kidding, right?"

He slanted his eyes at her. "What do you think?"

"You'd really rescue me, but you won't help me find Tara?"

"They're entirely two different things."

"How?"

He waited about two seconds, and then said, "Didn't we have an agreement about not socializing?"

Patience. The Lord was obviously teaching her patience. Or testing her faith. So Mallory didn't point out that Shamus had come to her first, nor that this was about a teenager's life, not going to lunch with the gang. She just drew a long breath and nodded solemnly at him, wanting badly to be an example of Christian patience after slipping so often lately.

"I'll be at my desk if you change your mind." She pushed until she was back in front of her computer and then stared at her screen as though she were really reading it instead of thinking. God wanted her to help Shamus, but God might well not want Shamus to help her. She was going to have to search for Tara alone.

. Not two seconds later, Shamus harrumphed a sigh, muttered something about meeting a probationer upstairs and strode from the room.

"Hmm. You really think that one is a nice guy?"

Mosey. Her gaze flew to her coworker. "Please don't say a word about the conversation you overheard to anyone, Mosey," she begged. "It has to do with a police investigation."

"Don't worry, I won't." Mosey leaned back in his chair, his hands clasped together behind his graying, curly dark brown hair. "But do you really think Shamus is worth all the effort you've been putting into him?"

"Yes," she said simply. "He brought your Santa back, didn't he?"

"Because you asked him to. He told me that. Made sure I knew he wouldn't have given it a second thought if you hadn't asked him to."

"He would have," she protested. She just knew it. Still, Mosey's doubt bothered her. Did no one besides her see the good in Shamus?

Mosey didn't argue. He said he had a home visit, so he grabbed his coat and took off, leaving Mallory to herself until the others showed up—or Shamus came back. She decided to grab the next hour while Bess was gone to look for Tara. She couldn't waste any time, not with the kidnapper running loose. As far as using work time for private purposes, she would work an extra hour that evening to make it up to the county.

She found and printed out the names of both of Tara's schools, current and earlier, hoping she could get a name of the friend who'd been at the pizza place with Tara. Then, instead of getting up and going, she stared at the screen, seeing Shamus's image in her mind.

It was comforting to know he would come rescue her again if she got into trouble she couldn't handle. There *was* a nice guy hidden under his pain.

But then, her mother had said the same thing about her father. Could she really count on Shamus? Should she?

Or was he the hypocrite Ginny claimed?

"Mallory, I could kill you! Are you all right?"

Startled, Mallory looked up at Ginny. She was dressed in elegant gray slacks and a dark blue silk top and looked relaxed, quite a change from Sunday.

"I'm fine. You heard about the Tripp shooting?"

"Top story in today's paper. Didn't take more than one call to get some particulars." Ginny leaned against Shamus's desk and stared at her so intently Mallory began to feel uncomfortable. Taking the sheet of paper containing Tara's schools, she folded it in half.

"I begged you to stay away from Burke," Ginny continued. "Now look. He dragged you into the middle of this, and you could have been killed."

"The sniper could have killed me anytime. Obviously, he wasn't after me."

"Oh, Mallory, can't you see? Burke has trouble written all over him. His wife dies, he either quits or gets fired from the police department—depending on which rumor you believe— and someone tries to blow up the office building Burke works in. And now he has someone shooting in his general direction. He's either a danger magnet or a modern-day Job."

"That doesn't mean I should abandon him," Mallory told her. "As a Christian, I need to help him if I can, and he needs a friend."

"I'm asking you again, Mal, please keep away from Shamus. It will be safer for you, and safer for us if we're going to be around you, especially outside working hours."

If? First Mosey and his doubts, and now Ginny was telling her to distance herself from Shamus and the bomber or risk everyone distancing themselves from her. Maybe that was why everyone had made themselves scarce. They were working on her one by one to get her to stop bothering with Shamus. Probably instigated by Ginny.

Before she got angry again, she told herself they meant well—they were worried about her being in danger. She wanted to smile and thank Ginny for her concern, but her jaw was stiff from tension.

"Sorry. I can't give up trying to help him." Picking up her sheet of paper with the addresses and her purse, Mallory headed for the coatrack by Ginny's desk. She needed to get over to the school before Bess returned. Every second she sat here was another second for the bomber to get to Tara.

Ginny rounded her desk and remained standing. "Please don't tell me you're falling for him," she said. "You've got to take off those rosy blinders you've been wearing since you got saved or Shamus Burke is going to make mincemeat out of your heart. He will. Believe me, I've been around the type. He's world-weary, cynical and detached, and he seems to like it that way."

"Actually, that description reminds me a little bit of you, Ginny," Mallory said in her most controlled voice, putting on her coat and pulling her hair free from the collar. She needed to get out of there before she screamed. Or cried.

"But you know what? Just like with Shamus, if you're ever down, I won't give up on you, either." Ready to leave, she looked right at Ginny, who looked as upset as she felt.

"If you'll excuse me, I have to go interview someone."

"You aren't going to look for Tara Tripp again, are you?"

The breath caught in Mallory's throat. There was only one way Ginny could know anything about that. "Mosey wasn't supposed to repeat what he heard."

"He's as worried about your safety—everyone's safety—as I am. Please don't go. If Tara really did escape, the bomber could be after her to shut her up."

Mallory slung her purse strap over her shoulder. "Tripp was the only family Tara had. Now she's out there all alone. I can't stand that." She didn't have to explain why—Ginny knew her history.

The other woman was struck speechless for a few seconds. "You *are* going to look for her."

What could she say? Turning, she headed out the door.

Ginny had just made it obvious that she couldn't count on anyone for help—not her best friend, or Mosey, or even, if she really thought about it, Shamus.

Oh, she had no doubt Shamus thought he was sincere when he said he would rescue her, but she remembered another set of eyes, the same color as her own, staring into hers as her brother told her he would rescue her from their home as soon as he got old enough. But then he'd gone off on his own, with just a note and probably not a second thought about her.

People meant well, but they considered themselves first. Shamus was nothing more than a stranger to her—she had no reason to believe he felt any obligation to her at all. She was being a silly romantic because a man had swept her away from danger twice. She really couldn't depend on people to rescue her ever. Only God. Hadn't she learned that already?

So she'd search for Tara alone. God would protect her. She didn't need Shamus.

Shamus walked quickly down the basement stairs to their makeshift office. The more time he had to think since Tripp's murder, the more he realized he needed to get loose of that woman. He was only putting her in danger. It was bad enough he was with her most of the day at work—to choose to be near her on his off-hours was the height of stupidity.

She apparently thought he had a heart worth saving—she was wrong. His heart was zapped into a shriveled little mass hidden somewhere deep inside him. The only way he could think of to convince her of that was to break his agreement to sing with the cantata.

Yeah. Let her bug him at work—he'd just continue to ignore her. He didn't have the heart to sing about Jesus' birth. He didn't have a heart at all.

Striding into the office, Shamus saw Mosey leaning over Jessica MacKenzie's desk, with Renzo nearby. They were deep in discussion, which stopped the second they noticed him. That didn't bother him. What did was a quick sweep of the room that told him Mallory's coat was no longer keeping his jacket warm, and she wasn't at her desk.

He scowled. She could be doing a home visit, but he had a feeling she wasn't. As per Bess's rule, home visits required two officers since Jessica had been taken captive by a probationer taking drugs the year before. Ginny was also there— he could hear her speaking with Bess in the cubicle where Bess's desk was.

He dropped his notes on the side of his desk and sat down to type them up. Wherever Mallory was, it wasn't his business.

"I thought you two were friends," Bess said on the other side of the screen. She was keeping her tone low, but there was no real privacy in their current setup. He tried not to listen as he raised his laptop screen.

"We are. I wouldn't be speaking to you about this if I wasn't worried to death about her," Ginny protested. "But if she's out there looking for Tara Tripp, which I'm fairly sure she is, she's putting herself in danger, and if the bomber is following her, the girl, too. Plus that, what if she angers the guy, and he follows her back here?"

Shamus gave up all pretense of not listening and sat back, the bottom part of his jaw moving back and forth.

"If you're so worried about her, why didn't you go with her as an extra set of eyes?" Bess asked. "You're armed."

Silence. Then, finally, "She and Burke were shot at by a sniper yesterday, Bess. None of us wants to go out with one of them under those circumstances. It's too dangerous."

That was enough for Shamus. He rolled back from his desk and rose to his feet. So Mallory's friends were all turning on her because she'd had the heart to want to give him a Christmas present but had picked the wrong day to stay late? And because she refused to abandon a homeless teenager none of them would touch?

He reached Bess's doorway in four steps.

"I'll go get her."

Ginny's eyes widened in surprise. She probably had counted on him not returning until after she was done snitching on her best friend.

Bess just turned her calm "I'm in control" gaze on him and nodded. "Fine. Go."

Shamus turned his scowl to Ginny. "As for the danger, it's me this bomber is after, or people I care about. I think you're safe enough."

"I didn't mean it that way," Ginny protested.

But he was already on his way to Mallory's desk to do a little detective work—minus the badge—and then to the coat rack, ignoring the sets of eyes he knew were watching him. He would have offered to work from home so they all wouldn't have to be so worried, but he wanted to stay in the office now. Someone had to look out for Mallory until the bomber was caught—even if he wasn't going to be her friend.

He'd just be her protector. Like he should have been there to protect his wife. He couldn't go everywhere with her, because he didn't want the bomber to think he was close to her, but he could follow her from a safe distance. That was after he hauled her back here today. He'd just tell Bess he'd be the one to partner with Mallory whenever she went out of the courthouse.

A plan, Shamus, he told himself. It was a plan.

Now he just had to figure out where she was.

SEVEN

So far, so good, Mallory thought as she waited for the vice-principal of Shepherd Falls High to get Tara's two friends out of their classes. The detective handling the Tripp murder had already done the investigative work and identified the teenagers earlier that morning in order to interview them. All Mallory did was tell the vice-principal she was Bud Tripp's probation officer, and he didn't even question her need to see them.

She was in his office, waiting for the man to return with the teenagers, when she heard a voice behind her.

"Busted."

She jumped up from her seat and whirled around to face Shamus. He was standing in the doorway, arms crossed, shaking his head at her.

"You startle easy."

A trait left over from growing up with her father. It only came back when she had a lot on her mind. "My nerves are on edge."

"Yeah. Breaking department rules will do that every time." He didn't look at all sympathetic.

"Does Bess know where I am?"

"She told me I should find you and bring you back to work."

"How did you know I was here?"

"Your computer. You left a high-school address highlighted when you printed it out."

"Good thing you weren't the bad guy, huh?"

Shamus didn't laugh. "Maybe you should save the jokes to humor Bess. She knows you went looking for Tara Tripp."

She really was in trouble. "Ginny told her?"

He looked so reluctant to reply, it couldn't have been anyone else. "It's okay, Shamus. Just please don't tell Bess where I am yet," she said in a low voice, just in case Vice-principal Fadowski or the secretary was entering the office. She couldn't tell, because she couldn't see past Shamus. "I have to talk to Tara's friends."

"Relax."

She had no idea what he meant by that, but it was too late to ask. She could hear Fadowski talking behind Shamus as he entered the outer office.

Shamus moved out of the doorway to her right, apparently planning to stay. She wasn't sure if that was good or bad. He was holding a bag in his hand, but she didn't have the opportunity to ask him what was in it.

"Ms. Larsen, these are Keisha Foster and Alexis Willoughby."

Alexis fit the description the guy at the pizza place had given Mallory, but she was careful not to react. Keisha, a stunning girl who could be a model, shifted the backpack she carried to her other hand and gave Mallory a measuring look that said she was short of the standards of anyone Keisha was willing to talk to. The teenager turned her focus to Shamus, and she gave him a sudden smile of recognition.

"Cookieman! What are you doin' here?" she asked. "My bro's not in trouble, is he?"

Mallory turned her gaze on Shamus. "Cookieman?"

"That's Probation Officer Cookieman to you, Ms. Larsen." Shamus didn't so much as grin at her. "Keish. No trouble, but I'd appreciate it if you help my friend."

To Mallory, Keisha's scowl did not look promising. On the other hand, Shamus was helping her, and quite possibly he would get through to the teenager. Amazing.

"Burke." Fadowski presented his hand to Shamus.

The two men shook hands, then Shamus held out a small bag from the coffee shop in Keisha's direction. Keisha grinned, grabbed the bag and opened it. The warm scent of chocolate drifted out, making Mallory's mouth water.

Cookieman. She glanced at Shamus. Imagine that.

"We're about to change classes in a few minutes," Fadowski said. "You can use my office." He shifted his gaze to the teenagers. "When they're done speaking with you, you girls go to your next class. Tell the teachers I kept you."

Fadowski strode away, and Shamus shut the office door.

There were seats along the wall, and Mallory swept her hand in that direction. When they were seated, Mallory took a deep breath.

"I'm Mallory Larsen. I was Tara's father's probation officer. I made him a deathbed promise that I would make sure Tara was safe, and I'm going to do that. So I need to know where she's hiding and how to get in touch with her."

Keisha took a round cookie with a fudge-covered top out of the bag Shamus had given her and handed it to Alexis. Alexis bit into it and chewed. Neither of them uttered a word as they ate their cookies, nor did they look at her.

Fine. It was time to get serious. Mallory grabbed the bag out of Keisha's hand and backed up.

"Hey! They're mine."

"You want them back, answer my question."

Sulking, Keisha turned to Shamus. "You were a cop. She stole something from me. Can't you get her arrested?"

"You're kidding, right? Answer Ms. Larsen's question." Shamus gave her the same narrow-eyed, intense gaze he'd been shooting at everyone for the past month. Mallory never would have guessed she'd be happy to see it back, but she was.

Keisha's mouth dropped open, and she swiveled around to stare at Alexis, who shook her head subtly, but enough to make Mallory wonder who was really in control.

"I have to tell," Keisha said to Alexis. "I don't want him to find a reason to revoke my brother's probation."

Alexis scowled, but it didn't stop Keisha from turning sullen eyes back to Mallory.

"Tara said if that guy finds her, he'll kill her. Because of what she knows."

"What did she mean by that?" Shamus asked sharply. Mallory could have sworn Keisha tensed up at his tone. Apparently, she really liked Shamus.

"I don't know what she meant," Keisha said. "But she's scared. She won't even tell us where she was gonna hide."

"What *did* she tell you?" Mallory asked.

"Nothing except she's safe and not to tell anyone anything about her."

"Which you did," Alexis said, irritation obvious in her voice. "If these two bring anyone down on her head, it's your fault."

Keisha's beautiful features crumpled, and Mallory felt her compassion kick in. "It isn't Keisha's fault," she told Alexis. "It's nobody's fault except the kidnapper's."

She handed the bag of cookies back to Keisha, who gripped the top shut with both hands.

"You need to tell us everything you know," Mallory said. "I can find Tara and make sure she stays safe."

Keisha looked at Shamus. "Can she do that?"

"Ms. Larsen will make sure she's safe. You can trust her."

Mallory could barely keep herself from showing surprise at his kind words, worried that doing so would distract the girls.

"She said she's not coming back here." Keisha jerked her

head to indicate the high-school grounds. "But she didn't say where she was going, honest."

"How do you contact her?" Shamus asked.

"She sends us emails." Keisha rattled off her e-mail address, and Mallory grabbed a pen and small reminder notepad from her purse to jot it down.

"What's her newest cell number?"

Keisha told her. "But if you call her, she'll just throw it away and get another one."

"Limitless money supply, hmm?" Credit cards were out; the police would be checking her father's for activity and surely Tara would know that and not use them. "Did she ever mention a boyfriend?"

Keisha shrugged. "She said she had one, but she wouldn't say who it was, so we figured she was lying to look popular. She said her father didn't want her to date."

"Tara is gonna *kill* you, Keisha," Alexis said, her voice filled with worry.

That didn't sound like the Tara she knew, so Mallory figured it was just the melodrama of teenagers. "I think Tara will end up being grateful someone cared enough about her to help."

"Whatever." Alexis rolled her eyes upward. "Can we go?" she asked.

Mallory gave a short nod, and watched as Alexis wasted no time getting out of there. When Mallory turned her gaze back to Keisha, the girl had grabbed her backpack, stood and was looking at Shamus.

"I don't know what's going on with Tara, but I have a funny feeling about it I can't explain. Watch your back, Cookieman."

With those words, she grabbed her bag of cookies and walked out of the offices into the hallway. Mallory turned back to Shamus, a question in her eyes. "Cookieman?"

"I got a 911 call once and walked in on her father beating

her when she was eight. I stopped it. Put her father in jail, got her mother into a safe-harbor house and brought her cookies in the hospital until she got out. I made it a point to check on her every so often since, and always brought her cookies. She must still have a soft spot for me."

No one who would remember a little girl for all those years could be a hypocrite. She could at least put that worry to rest. But something else didn't make sense. "How did you know already she'd be one of Tara's friends?"

"I didn't."

"Sure, Shamus. You just carry a bag of cookies around with you…"

He sent her an intense gaze that haunted her for a few seconds until finally, she understood his unspoken message.

"They were for me?" she asked softly.

"We have to talk, and you aren't going to like what I have to say. I thought cookies would soften the blow."

Her lips parted in a slow smile. "You brought cookies just for me?"

"Yes, but not because I want to be friends—"

"Shamus, that was a really sweet thing to do." She started buttoning her coat as she headed out the first office door into the outer office.

She wasn't getting away so easily this time. Right behind her, Shamus caught her arm before she got beyond the door into the hallway that was crowded with teenagers changing classes, making her turn around.

"Don't you want to know what we have to talk about?" he asked.

"No," she said gently. "You said I wouldn't like it, and right now, I'm coping with enough. As soon as I have the time and energy to be upset with whatever you have to tell me, I'll let you know."

She'd let him know. That should have irritated him more than he already was with her for taking off after Tara Tripp. But she wasn't trying to be arrogant—she was just trying to cope with a life that had turned suddenly ugly. He understood that.

Boy, did he understand that.

"Why aren't you angry with Ginny?"

"She's my friend. All of them are. I can understand why she went to Bess—she's scared for me and herself and the others. I forgive her."

Her ability to maintain a Christian attitude was amazing. But he'd have to think about that later.

"So you're going back to work now, right?"

Her face was apologetic. "Sorry, Shamus, I can't. Not quite yet. I'm going to spot check Tripp's house first on the off chance Tara is hiding in plain sight."

"If I did that for you, then would you go back to work?"

Mallory considered it. "Not a good idea. If Tara is there, she might well be traumatized by a strange male. But she's met me and knows I'm not a threat. So, no. I need to do it."

"You heard what Keisha said about whatever is going on here—that something doesn't seem quite right to her? What if Tara is the threat?"

"I'm not my brother. I made a promise to her father, and I'm going to keep it. No matter who it angers, or what it costs." She shook her head and looked through the office doorway to the hall with its lockers, remembering the past. Feeling the hurt of those years all over again when Ethan had broken his promise and left her behind. "I can't let Tara think no one cares."

The roar from the students changing classes was quieting. Shamus eyed the door and made what he had to say short and sweet.

"You're right about no one caring like you will, but the

reality I figured out when I was a cop is that there are some people who don't want to be helped. Tara purposely took off on her own instead of letting you help her. Some people are perfectly happy messing up their own lives."

Might as well get it over with, now that he'd led himself right into his bad news for her. "That's why I've changed my mind about singing in the cantata."

Her deep green eyes lost none of their warmth, and she reached up and brushed at his coat sleeve. "All I know, Shamus, is that you can run away from the cantata, but you can't run fast enough to get away from God."

He paused for long seconds. Her faith was so strong. He couldn't even come close. That was how she remained so positive, even when people were putting her through pain.

"I don't have to run from God, Mallory. He's avoiding me right now. All the prayers in the world haven't helped me with the feeling He's punishing me for putting my job before my wife's safety. I can't sense Him anywhere." And he'd been trying to, so hard.

"He wouldn't abandon you," Mallory told him, her voice full of assurance. "He has a reason. Sometimes we have to wait to find out."

The secretary walked in and took her place behind the long counter, followed by the vice-principal with an angry parent. The roar in the hallway had lessened to barely distinguishable voices passing by. Mallory glanced at the doorway and back to Shamus.

"I'd be happy to talk about this more later." Her rose-colored lips parted in a smile. "And I'll make sure I tell Bess you really tried, Shamus. I promise."

Somehow, that didn't make him feel better as he watched her leave the office. He didn't really care what Bess thought of him, but he did care about Mallory. He didn't want to, but he did.

He didn't want to chance endangering her any more than he already had by talking to her here, so he gave her a couple of minutes to reach her car before he moved to the glass-door entrance. When she pulled out of her parking space, he pushed through the doors. Less than two minutes later he was on the main road, heading toward a small, modest subdivision and Tripp's home, having looked up the address the first night after the bombing.

He wished he could believe Mallory, that God hadn't abandoned him. For the long year he'd searched for his wife's murderer, he hoped he would sense God in his life again after he was done. But even after the man's arrest, all his faith was still knotted up inside of him, covered with a rock-hard coating of guilt.

But whether God was with him or not, or existed or not, he wasn't going to make the same mistake of not being there for a woman he cared about twice. If Mallory was too stubborn to give up her search for Tara, he would just have to be her shadow, hang in the distance and watch over her. That way, if the bomber did follow her, he'd be able to see who it was before the person could hurt someone else because of him.

His thoughts too troubling, Shamus turned his attention to Bud Tripp's choice of a better neighborhood for his daughter. The homes were modest, but the sidewalks were well-shoveled, and quite a lot of the lawns were decorated for Christmas. As he watched for Pine Street, he saw everything from a towering plastic snowman that seemed almost as big as the one-story home behind it, to a light-strewn Santa complete with sleigh and reindeer. The neighborhood seemed warm and almost comforting—was it enough to draw Tara Tripp home?

He turned down Pine and stopped at the head of the street. There were quite a few cars around, parked in driveways and on the street. Good. He'd be less conspicuous that way. Mallory's SUV was only two houses down, parked facing him. She wasn't in it, so she must have gone inside.

He didn't want her to spot him on her way back to work, so he backed up, circled the block and approached from the other direction, the whole time watching for anyone sitting in a parked car who might be following Mallory. All was quiet.

He parked three houses down behind her. When he'd made detective, he'd chosen a vehicle that looked like dozens of others on purpose—a casual glance his way wouldn't raise Mallory's suspicions unless she spotted him.

It only took a minute for something to start to happen. Even as he watched, he wasn't sure what he was seeing. Maybe it was nothing, but instinct had him tense and reach for his weapon.

Then the figure walked across the Tripp lawn instead of continuing down the sidewalk, heading toward the back of the house, and Shamus launched himself out of the car at a run.

EIGHT

Since the back door was unlocked and the house was one story with two bedrooms, it only took Mallory a couple of minutes to check everywhere. No sign of Tara, but she definitely *had* been back since the kidnapping. Her closet and her dresser drawers were empty, and the top of her bureau was bare. All that was left in the house was whatever had belonged to Bud Tripp that the police hadn't taken to try to solve his murder.

Disappointed, Mallory turned toward the kitchen to leave. That's when the pounding at the front door started.

Her knees went weak. Her throat became a desert. Everyone who'd tried to warn her was right, and she was dead wrong. She was an idiot for coming here alone.

Running to the back door, she slipped outside and ran around the side of the house to peer around the corner.

"Shamus!" she said in astonishment.

He had his leg readied to kick down the door. Instead, he jumped over the railing and made a dash through the snow for her, grabbing her hand and pulling her toward the street. There was only one reason she could think of that would make him hurry away from the house like this.

Another bomb. *Please, Lord, not another bomb.*

Breathless, her heart pounding all over again, she raced down the street with him until they reached his car. She slid into the passenger's side and he into the driver's side, his gaze taking in his surroundings. She kept her eyes on the Tripp home, expecting it to explode into flames.

"What happened?" she asked as soon as he started the car.

"Someone was headed toward the back of the house. He saw me and fled, so keep your eyes out for anyone on foot. Mallory, I told you messing with this guy could be dangerous."

"Then why didn't you go after him?"

He gave her one short glance as he drove, slowly, down the street. Instead of the irritation she thought she'd see in his eyes, there was fear.

"I had to get you to safety," he said, his usually strong voice shaky. "I didn't know if he'd planted a bomb, or had a friend in there holding you hostage. I just had to make sure you were all right."

"Shamus." She reached over and squeezed his arm gently. "It's okay to care about someone, you know."

"Yeah, so then you're my responsibility and I can mess up again? No, thanks." He shook his head. "Tell me if you see anyone on foot."

One look at Shamus's clenched jaw told her now was not the time to debate with him. "What did the guy look like?" she asked, leaning forward as she scanned the homes.

"Santa."

"You're kidding." But no, he gave her one of his no-nonsense looks. His normal look, really. "What am I saying? Of course you're not kidding. How do you know he was dangerous?" she asked. "What if he was just some nice guy collecting for a charity?"

"What if he was someone the bomber sent to follow you in disguise?" he countered.

"Oh," she whispered. "I guess that might have been a close one, huh?"

"I'd say. Think back. Have any sidewalk Santas paid you a lot of attention before or after the bombing?"

Before, no. After? She scrunched her forehead, trying to think. Finally, she shook her head. "I don't know. Seems like there's a Santa everywhere lately. Have *you* noticed anything off with any of them?"

"I wasn't paying attention to anything Christmas."

"Until now."

He glanced at her and nodded in agreement. "Until now."

He had looked at her in *that* way again, and she blushed and turned her attention to their search. About two minutes later, after seeing no one, Shamus parked his car behind hers, undid his seat belt and faced her.

"When I followed you, I was hoping to sit here and not see a soul except you walking back out to your car. Then I was going to return to work and ignore you."

"Funny. I was hoping for the same thing—to go back to work and ignore you," she said. "But not until after you sang in the cantata."

Was she serious? She wanted to ignore him?

"Well, it turns out I can't ignore you. A strange man showing up at the same house as you—I'm taking it as a sign that you need protection. I'll have to be part of the cantata after all, so I'm nearby to watch out for you. I'll also be following you until the police catch this guy. I just wanted to tell you so I won't take you by surprise."

Now she was smiling. "What you're really saying is that you've decided to stop running."

Her positive spin on everything was driving him nuts. "No, what I'm really saying is that I'm not letting you be on the streets alone while the guy after me is loose."

"Different words, same result."

She needed to face the cold reality of his situation. "Don't expect anything out of me, Mallory. You're going to end up disappointed. I'm going to the cantata practices so you don't end up dead, that's all."

"Okay," she said solemnly.

"Your eyes are twinkling. Mine aren't."

"I know," she assured him. "I'm glad you're coming, whatever the reason."

"I give up." He threw his hands out.

"Are we going to report this?" she asked him.

"Report what? I saw a man in a Santa suit headed for the Tripp house. Take it from a former detective—it's a nonevent. The only one who's suspicious of it is me."

"Us," she corrected. "But I guess you're right. There's no point. By now he could be out of the suit and unidentifiable."

"Right. So did you find anything the police missed when you were inside the house?"

"I don't know when they were last here, but it's obvious Tara has been back to move out permanently. Everything of hers I saw on my last home visit is gone, even her hardcover book collection."

"So she's staying someplace with a lot of room to store her things. Someplace safe. Which means she doesn't need your help anymore." And that he wouldn't have to worry about her dashing off after work hours to look for Tara.

"We don't know that. She could have put her things in storage and be hiding out under a bridge."

"A suspicious Santa, evidence that Tara is just fine—nothing's going to stop you from searching for her, is it?"

"I can't," she said, putting her hands in front of the heater vents. "I feel as though I'm being called to find this girl, Shamus, and I need to find her fast." She turned her gentle eyes on him. "I'm sorry. I know you have a lot of worries right now, and I'm just one more. But I have a strong sense that finding Tara is a lot more important than either of us realize."

By the time they got back to work, Bess was pacing the office, and not in her usual, good way. She put her hands on her hips as Mallory and Shamus walked in.

"Larsen, Burke, hang up your coats and follow me." She disappeared into the hallway.

Mallory sought out Shamus's eyes, and he gave her an "I warned you" look. She then offered Ginny a toned-down smile, lest Bess think she thought being summoned by her boss was funny. Her friend turned away and started typing again without saying a word.

By now, Mallory had hoped Ginny would have thought twice about threatening her with isolation. Stupid her. She looked at each of her coworkers' desks, but the only one who met her eyes was Mosey, and even he looked grim.

Hurt saturated every part of her even as she reminded herself once again that she understood everyone's fear. Shamus touched her arm and gave her a reassuring look, just as Bess circled back in from the hallway.

"I'm still waiting, and that's not good," she warned.

Mallory pushed her hurt aside. She might as well get it over with. Even though she'd never been the target of it before, Bess's yelling couldn't be any worse than losing her friends.

The chief probation officer took them up the stairs into one of the small meeting rooms that held a table and a few simple chairs and shut the door with a slam. Bess was just under average height with a slim build, but she had a "no prisoners taken" personality that made people pay attention to her.

At least, Mallory did.

"Larsen, just what were you thinking?"

Her boss's sharp gaze made Mallory wince. No sense in pretending she didn't know precisely what Bess was referring to. "I promised Bud Tripp right before he died that I would find his daughter and make sure she was safe. She escaped from the kidnapper and is in hiding, and I was trying to get a lead on where she might be."

"Vice-Principal Fadowski called to tell me you'd been there." Bess continued to stare at her. "And then you went somewhere else that I don't want to know about, but I can guess it concerned the same girl. Mallory, Tara Tripp is not your probationer. You interfered with a police investigation by questioning her friends."

Shamus had picked a chair at the far end of the small conference table, so he couldn't see Mallory that well, as she was facing Bess. But Mallory wasn't defending herself. She should. She'd only been trying to do what she considered the right thing, and here she was getting it from all sides. He had to do something.

"Bess," he said, "I have some experience in the field of police investigations."

Mallory turned all the way around to look at him, her eyes widening in surprise that he was getting into the middle of her problem. Bess, on the other hand, didn't seem the least bit shocked he would interfere.

"Do tell, Burke," she said.

"Since the police had already spoken with Tara's friends, I wouldn't call Mallory's questions interfering."

Bess didn't say anything for quite a few seconds as she considered this. Then she turned her gaze back to Mallory.

"I guess he just saved you. But you need to stop pursuing this during working hours, or I'm going to have to suspend you."

Again, Mallory didn't say anything.

"She won't do it again," Shamus said, and Mallory turned

and mouthed, "Yes, I will." But their boss did not see it, so he let it go.

"Hmm," Bess said, looking from him to Mallory and back. "To clarify, I consider searching for Tara Tripp private business, not probation business. If you don't have enough work to do, I'm sure I can come up with more cases for you."

Mallory nodded solemnly.

"Now there's this matter of your coworkers worrying about the danger to them after the bombing last Friday. Burke, do the police think the bombing was about you somehow?"

"Yeah. It's leaning that way."

Bess pursed her lips. "Knowing how the others feel, are you comfortable working from here, or would you prefer working from home?"

"I'll stay here," Shamus told her. He could keep tabs on Mallory better if he was near her. And a work setting was the only one that wouldn't scream "personal interest in her" to the bomber.

He supposed if he just disappeared, everything would settle down, but he couldn't do that. What if Mallory needed him? Make that needed him *again?* Today was the third time in five days. The odds seemed good that she would.

"Burke, you're carrying, right?" Bess asked.

Shamus nodded.

"You two double up on any home visits you need to make. Shamus drives. I'm assuming that's not a problem for you?"

Shamus shook his head. When Mallory left the office, it would save him having to make excuses so he could follow her.

Mallory didn't like this at all. She wouldn't be able to get out of the office alone during work hours if she got a lead on Tara. Except for lunch hour. But she couldn't think of a thing she could do about it.

"We all done?" Shamus asked, starting to rise.

"One more thing," Bess said sternly, pushing a strand of jet-black hair that slipped down around her chin behind her ears. "I have a feeling you won't care, Shamus, but I'll say this anyway. Watch out. You aren't above the rules, either." She pinned him with her eyes. "Now," she said with a dramatic pause, "we're all done."

Striding out, she left them behind. Mallory rose and turned to Shamus, who had come to the front of the room.

"Thank you. You stood up for me, and that's the last thing I expected."

"Why? You never do anything out of selfish motives. You didn't this morning. Why wouldn't you expect someone to stick up for you?"

Mallory decided to be honest. "Because no one ever has before. And because you put your own career at risk."

He shrugged. "I don't know if you've noticed, but I'm not in love with this job. It wasn't a big sacrifice."

"Yes, it was. It's all you have."

Shamus knew that, but he'd never thought of it as a negative before. He liked having one thing to throw himself into. That way, he wouldn't have to deal with anything else in his life. But all that had changed, anyway.

"Wrong," he told her. "Ever since you tapped Santa's head last Friday, I've had two things I've been focused on—my work…and you. I'm just trying to figure out how in the world I let that happen, because messing up your life is the last thing I want."

He left the room, leaving Mallory with wide eyes. She already had figured out he cared about her. No man would do all he had if he didn't care. But what he'd just said sounded more like…like he cared about her in a *romantic* way. Was that what he meant by messing up her life?

It couldn't be. He probably just meant that his being around her was causing the others in the office to avoid her, and that was messing up her previously happy life. She was going with that interpretation, because his thinking romance would really mess up her life…and that was the last thing she wanted.

Or was it? For a long minute, she pictured his dark-eyed gazes that sent her heart skipping every time he looked at her. And thought about how the mere sight of him made her want to smile because she felt secure whenever he was around. He was brave, he'd come through for her time after time, and he'd stood up for her.

What's not to like, Mallory?

That he was going to the cantata rehearsal only to watch over her, not to sing for God? That he was not going to help her find Tara, even if he stood up for her and protected her while she worked on it? Shamus Burke had a strong sense of duty, perhaps brought on by his guilty feelings over his wife, but he'd lost his heart.

If her efforts to get him reinvolved in life didn't work, he could well remain the unhappy recluse that he was. She couldn't chance getting all emotional about him. She would not be her mother all over again, trying to make a man happy who was determined not to be.

If Shamus didn't get the joy back in his life after the cantata, she needed to withdraw from him totally—even if it meant cutting the strings of friendship they had. She might even have to start stepping back emotionally now, before she got in too deep.

Because getting in too deep with Shamus would be a disaster.

Wednesday's workday passed with no answers to Mallory's e-mails and calls to Tara's cell phone, no news on the bomber and no attempt on Ginny's part to make the slightest bit of conversation. She and Shamus were both keeping their distance, which left Mallory feeling alone in a room filled with people. When five o'clock came, she was out of there, happy to grab a quick bite to eat and then get to the church early for the cantata practice.

Tucked into a corner of the meet and greet room, where people stashed their coats on a big table and got coffee and a snack before the practice, Mallory checked her phone messages—still nothing. Earlier, she'd tried to find out about the boyfriend Tara might have had by calling Tara's previous high school, but the principal had been told to clam up for Tara's safety by Dickerson, the lead detective on the Tripp murder case. Well, fine. That left her free for the time being to work on helping Shamus.

He was right inside the door, where he'd been besieged since he'd arrived by people welcoming him back. The crowd had thinned and the room was fairly quiet, but she was going to give him another minute to get his bearings and deal with the memories he had to be having of being there with his deceased wife, what with her dad, Paul McCauley, now talking to him.

"I'm surprised to see you back in church, Shamus," Paul said. "I'd thought you'd given up on God."

Shamus winced. Assuming Paul would be there, as the original cantata organizer, he'd tried to come up with something in advance to say to him. But there was no way to really prepare for coming face-to-face with the father of the woman whose death you felt responsible for.

Silence hung between them. The few people around them watched, their collective breaths held. And then Shamus smelled apples and cinnamon wafting beside him.

"Please don't scare him off, Mr. McCauley," Mallory said, giving him one of her bright smiles. "Our bass section is woefully small."

"She's got a point, Paul." John Tabor, one of the elders, gave him a friendly slap on the back. "We need all the help we can get."

Ruth's father shook his head, as if to clear away bad memories, and waved his hand. "I apologize," he told Shamus. "Didn't mean anything by it. Ruth would have been pleased you've returned."

As the older man walked off toward the hallway leading to the sanctuary, where they would be practicing, people started following him out. Shamus turned to Mallory.

"Thank you," he said, meaning it, "for getting me here." For getting him through his first meeting with his former father-in-law since the funeral, he meant, but he couldn't say that where anyone could overhear.

"Anytime." She started to turn away, but then her eyes lit up, and he could tell she was holding back a smile.

"Shamus! You're wearing the scarf I made you."

He was. He'd gotten home from work and sat there for an hour, alone, telling himself Mallory would be fine at the church and there was no real need to go to the rehearsal after all. He'd stared at the tattered gift, and it reminded him that she'd been likewise battered by the blast. Angry with himself for putting her in danger, he'd ripped what remained of the wrapping paper off the box, only to find an old-fashioned Santa Claus staring up at him, reminding him of when he'd been a kid. Suddenly he'd wanted to see what Mallory had given him for Christmas.

And after he'd opened the box and admired the scarf he'd wanted to wear it, because he'd known it would make her happy, even if he was detaching himself from her.

"You did a good job," he told her. "The yarn is soft." Like Mallory herself. "I like the blue shades you used."

"You have three shirts in the darkest blue, so I guessed you might like it," she teased, happiness lighting her eyes. She tugged at the collar of his leather jacket. "You should take your jacket off, Shamus. You look ready to run."

He wasn't, but he didn't tell her that. No sense in letting her get any wrong ideas about him coming back after the cantata. He shed his coat, wishing he'd been able to bring his weapon inside. But this was a church, and he didn't feel right about it.

They could hear the pianist warming up in the sanctuary. Mallory glanced around them, saw that they were almost alone, and said softly, "I know you don't think God is listening, but maybe while you're singing to Him, He'll hear your heart."

Hadn't he been praying all this time, hoping precisely that? Why would God suddenly listen now? He would have asked, but she headed out of the room.

He waited a minute and then walked to the sanctuary and up the three steps onto the pulpit that had been cleared for the practice, standing where Paul indicated, in the back row. Mallory was in the front row on the opposite side.

Their first song was "Joy to the World," and by the time they finished working on that, he had to admit his shoulders felt looser than they had in months.

As they were starting the second song, one of the doors at the far end of the sanctuary opened and a blond-haired man who could have played fullback for some football team entered. Luke Cramer. Shamus's shoulders tensed back up as Luke stripped off his bomber jacket, tossed it on top of the nearest pew, flew up the stairs and headed right toward...

Mallory.

"Miss me?" he asked, giving her a quick hug and then moving behind her into the tenor section.

Shamus's eyes narrowed. He watched Mallory turn her head just enough so that he caught a half smile she gave Cramer that he'd never seen on her face before. He'd seen her happy, and that look was not it. Yet she didn't look unhappy, either.

Was this the guy she had mentioned seeing? Luke Cramer? He sincerely hoped not. Shamus wanted to go over there, pluck her out of the choir line and out of Cramer's gaze. He was certain she had no idea about Cramer, but he would enlighten her as soon as possible.

He wasn't jealous. He wasn't going near that kind of relationship with Mallory, and he had no right thinking that way. He did consider her a friend, though, and the idea that she dated Luke, even casually, worried him through the rest of the songs. Two were new, and he should have been focusing, but he kept watching Mallory to see if she would grin up at Cramer again.

She didn't, but by the time practice was over and people moved off the stage, his shoulders were as locked up as his heart was. It didn't help that Mallory was heading right toward him, Luke in tow.

"Shamus, I want you to meet a good friend of mine—"

"Luke Cramer. Yeah, we've met."

Mallory's eyebrows dipped as she frowned. Shamus told himself to stop watching her. For all he knew, Luke Cramer could be the man behind the bombing and trying to make his life miserable. He didn't want Cramer to find out he liked her.

He took a deep breath. And it was possible, he conceded, he wasn't being fair. Maybe the man had changed. After all, *he* had changed since the last time the two of them had tangled with each other three years ago.

"Burke," Cramer acknowledged with a dip of his head. "Mallory tells me you two are working in the same office."

"That's right."

Mallory frowned at Shamus, whose whole demeanor had changed since she'd last glanced at him during one of the songs. Before he'd been almost peaceful, enjoying the singing. Now he was staring at Luke as if a snake had just slithered up on the pulpit and was about to strike.

Something must have happened between them, but what? She doubted Luke had gotten into any trouble with the law. Not even a rumor about anything bad about him had ever reached her. She couldn't imagine what had gotten into Shamus, but it was obvious Luke and he weren't going to become friends as she had hoped.

"Just call me jealous, then," Luke said, his smile looking forced. "I'd love to work in the same office as Mallory."

Shamus turned and headed toward the pulpit steps. Mallory's gaze followed him. Every inch of her wanted to chase after him, but how would that look if the bomber had a spy here? She'd have to ask him what was wrong later. If Luke was going to keep him from attending practice, she didn't know what she was going to do.

"Are you free for dinner Friday night?" Luke asked.

She moved her attention back to her friend just in time to catch the hard look on his face changing back to his normal, carefree expression.

"Why did Shamus act like that toward you?" And why were you so angry yourself just now?

Luke shrugged his wide shoulders. If she hadn't caught his chameleon change, she would have believed he was totally unconcerned about Shamus. "We had a minor misunderstanding a few years ago," he told her. "No big deal to me, but apparently he's still irritated."

Apparently. And she wanted to know why.

"So how about dinner Friday?" he asked.

"I'll have to let you know." She wanted to talk to Shamus first. "If you'll excuse me, I need to check on something."

"I'll come with you," he said. "I've got nothing else to do."

That was the last thing she wanted. "No, thank you. I'll call you if I can make dinner," she promised, reaching up to give him a reassuring pat.

Mistaking her intention, he leaned forward and pulled her to him for a few seconds. She patted his back, drew herself away and headed toward the rear door to see if she could catch up with Shamus before he went outside to his car. She needed to make sure he wasn't giving up on the cantata.

Pausing at the doorway, she turned suddenly and checked the room over her shoulder to see if anyone was focused on her. No one was, not even Luke, who had grabbed his jacket and was pulling it on as he strode toward the front of the sanctuary at top speed.

Odd, considering he'd just told her he had nothing else to do. That had certainly changed in a hurry, and she found that as disturbing as Shamus had seemed to find Luke.

She needed to tell him.

Shamus hadn't wanted to talk to Paul McCauley again, but he'd stomped off from Luke and Mallory, entered the coat room, and there the man had been, pulling on his own jacket.

Ruth's father had grayed considerably from two years ago, and sadness shrouded his face. But the eyes he raised to meet Shamus's gaze were hard and assessing. Still, Shamus preferred them to Luke Cramer's lying ones.

"Paul," Shamus acknowledged, walking over to take his jacket and scarf from the table. He would have left the room without another word, but Paul stopped him.

"You know I was dead set against Ruth marrying you. You were a cop. I never liked cops."

Shamus admitted something he never thought he would to the man. "I should have quit the force when she asked me to."

"You should have." The man nodded slowly. Tears filled

his eyes, but they never lost their hardness. "You did convince her to sing in the cantata. That was good—I loved hearing her sing. But she'd still be here now if you had only done what she'd asked." Without buttoning up his heavy woolen coat, Paul walked out of the room.

Shamus closed his eyes and shook his head slowly, his heart heavy once more with guilt.

"Shamus," Mallory's gentle voice said.

He blinked and left his eyes open. Mallory was in front of him, her face filled with sympathy. "You were enjoying yourself out there. Don't let what Paul said change that."

At the sight of her, some of the pain inside left him. She wanted to help him so much. He appreciated that. He'd never met anyone like her.

"I won't quit," he said. He couldn't. He had to stay near her. To protect her. No matter what the cost.

"Good." Mallory could feel the difference in him, but she couldn't tell exactly what it was. "Very good." She reached for her coat, and before she knew it, he had taken it himself and was helping her on with it.

She cast an anxious glance toward the door, but no one was watching, and she let herself enjoy his efforts to be nice.

Then she remembered her other reason for finding him.

"Luke took off really fast all of a sudden," she told him, "after saying he had nothing to do. Since you don't appear to like him much, I thought that would interest you." She paused for two beats of her heart, her eyes on the door, just in case someone came for their coat. "So why don't you like him?"

"He's a past problem. Don't go anywhere alone with him, Mallory."

"Why?"

He didn't want to get into it here, where someone could overhear. "For now, just take my word for it, please?"

Shamus was holding back, but if she pushed, she'd get nowhere—she already knew that much about him. So she decided she didn't need to know what kind of problem, since Luke was also a present solution.

"Whatever you say." She had what she wanted, which was Shamus's promise to stay in the cantata. "And don't you worry about Paul and Luke anyway, Shamus. I'm here with you." She grabbed his fingers and held his hand. "I won't let them hurt you, I promise."

At her touch, warmth flooded his iced-over veins. Their eyes connected, and something in Shamus gave way. He leaned down and met her lips with his, briefly. Then again, and they lingered there as he kissed her. And all the while her hand held his, her soft skin warming his heart, reminding him of how nice it was to really care about someone—and have them care back.

They both heard the door click shut and jolted apart. Mallory backed away, and the only thing that registered in Shamus's mind was how huge and beautiful her eyes were.

"Uh-oh." She hurried to open the door and check the fellowship hall. The elderly Mrs. Lansdale was just coming out of the ladies' room. Not her. Her gaze hit the rear exit, just in time to see the side of what looked like a red-and-white suit.

"Shamus, Santa!"

He joined her in two seconds, and together they hurried to open the heavy door and continue outside onto the shoveled sidewalk.

Santa was running to a late-model car and getting in, but the car was at an angle and too far away for her to read the license number. She would have run closer to him, but Shamus put both hands on her upper arms to restrain her.

"He could have a gun," he said, "and I don't have mine. Let's get back inside."

"Wait." It didn't look like Santa was going to stick around and be a problem, and she needed to ask him something now that she was positive they were alone. "Why did you kiss me?"

"I don't know."

"And I don't know why I kissed you back, Shamus." She shrugged helplessly. "But I do know that Santa saw us. You have to start figuring out who he is, Shamus. You can't just sit around and let him hurt you or hurt me, not when you're finally starting to rebuild your life."

He could not start hunting someone down again. Going after the bomber himself would mean waking up his emotions, and he didn't want to do that. It hurt too much. He had all he could do to deal with whatever it was he was feeling for Mallory while he kept her safe.

"*If* I were rebuilding something, you'd be right. I'm not. I'm not sorry I kissed you, but we can't do that again, and we both know it. I just forgot for a few seconds that you were untouchable. I won't forget it again."

He was fighting being happy with everything he had, Mallory thought. And she found herself getting angry, an emotion she didn't want to deal with.

"Fine. But you're wrong, Shamus," she said, starting to shiver. "God doesn't want you to be punished. It's you who wants it."

Leaving him, she walked resolutely toward the rear door to go inside for her coat and purse. Shamus didn't follow. She wasn't giving up on him—she'd promised God. No, what she was going to do was go home and have a good cry, because he was right. There couldn't be any more kissing between them. He was definitely all wrong for her.

At least she didn't have to worry about her safety. If the bomber came near her, she could tell him with certainty that Shamus had absolutely no feelings for her. Shamus was only looking for the forgiveness he thought he needed from God by protecting her. What she was starting to feel for him wouldn't be returned, and she had to watch her heart.

Which had already gotten her too carried away.

NINE

Mallory went to bed with aching eyes from crying, but new resolve. She was letting all of this ruin her Christmas, the most precious time of year for her. No more. She was going to search for Tara with courage and conviction, ditch her anger and be nice to everyone, no matter how they acted to her.

As for Shamus, she planned business as usual. If he didn't want to fight back against the attack on his life, fine. He didn't care enough yet about life. She just needed to keep working on him, trust God and not mind so much when he came down like a brick to smash her hopes for him. It wasn't going to be easy, but it had to be that way.

Thursday morning, armed with her new plan to find Tara, Mallory got on the road early, dressed in her warmest pant suit, her beige coat and a dark green, knit hat that matched her eyes. Twenty minutes later, she was in the neighborhood Bud Tripp had stolen money to get out of. It was an area no one would want to go to, and using a teenage girl's logic, maybe that would be the very place Tara chose to hide out.

By 8:45 a.m., Mallory decided knocking on doors was hopeless. Only three people on Tara's street said they knew her, and they all denied seeing any trace of the teenager for months.

She also checked out the former Tripp house itself. The

snow was trampled down in places, but there was a kids' ball left near the bushes, and that could account for that. It was hard to say if anyone was hiding inside without going inside, and she wasn't about to try that. Too much to explain if one of the neighbors called the police. And too dangerous.

She got to her office by fifteen after nine, a little late, but only Shamus and Jessica were there, and she knew Shamus wouldn't report her tardiness. He gave her a long look but didn't say a word, because, really, what was there to say?

At noon, she slipped off to eat alone in the courthouse cafeteria, and when she returned, only Mosey was at his desk. She'd always thought of him as a father figure, almost from the beginning of working there, and was relieved when he gave her a big smile when she came in. She hadn't had an opportunity to say more than a couple of words to him since Tuesday, but it looked like everyone else was still out to lunch, so she headed to his desk and leaned down so she couldn't be overheard. If anyone came into the room suddenly.

"You're not mad at me, too?"

"Of course not, sweetheart. None of this is your fault. Not to worry."

She was so relieved that someone besides Shamus was okay with her, she decided to forgive him for telling Ginny she was going to search for Tara two days ago, and went to her workstation. Where she would work, she promised Bess silently.

After she checked her e-mail again for word from Tara.

Bess came in, along with Shamus, and she tried to pretend he wasn't there. And that the nearby heating vent wasn't somehow blowing the spicy scent of his cologne over to where she was. And that he hadn't said a word to her.

Sighing, she refocused on Tara.

Even if the teenager was hiding in her old neighborhood, Mallory wasn't going to find out without sitting in her vehicle and watching the area. Which would be way too dangerous. And she had no other leads.

A little of her resolve started to slip. She needed a sign from God that she was supposed to persevere in helping Shamus— not that she was helping him—and finding Tara—not that she was doing that, either. Because what if her feelings were wrong? What if she was supposed to be ignoring Shamus and letting the police handle Tara's disappearance?

Shaking herself mentally, she took a deep breath. This wasn't her way. She was not her father, always pessimistic. She lived her life knowing God was in control and had beaten the doom-and-gloom thing long ago. Why was it coming back now?

Shamus—and the kiss they'd shared. The kiss had ruined everything. It had made her think they were closer than they really were. She had to remember—it was just a kiss, not a commitment.

Work. Lifting her purse to put into her desk drawer, she noticed a piece of mail addressed to her that must have come in during the lunch hour.

From its shape, it could be a Christmas card from a proba-tioner. She didn't recognize the address, but that didn't mean anything with her workload.

But maybe—could it be from Tara?

Filled with hope, carefully preserving the return address, she pulled the loosely sealed flap free from the envelope. A little bit of glitter fell out, and she almost smiled. She loved Christmas cards with glitter.

She turned the card to open it and check the signature, but the front picture caught her eye, and she froze.

Santa stood in the middle of a city street that was already white with snow, looking very merry and happy at the flakes coming down. At his feet was what looked like a computer-generated overlay of a sketch of a woman. A woman with reddish-brown hair in long curls and a fur collar on a beige coat. There was no doubt in Mallory's mind who the woman was supposed to be.

Her.

And there, on the ground next to her, was a pool of blood.

"Shamus!" Her voice sounded so strangled she thought he couldn't possibly have heard her, so she opened her mouth to try again. But he was already at her side, carefully lifting the card by its edges out of her trembling hands. Mosey also got up and strode to her desk. He was joined by Tony Renzo, who'd just returned.

But the only man Mallory could focus on was Shamus, who had put the card on the table and was opening it by its edges.

"'Stop looking for Tara Tripp, or else,'" he read out loud. He let go of the top, which dropped down so that the card was once again closed.

Mosey reached forward, but Shamus shook his head. "Don't touch. It's evidence."

She gazed up at Shamus. Anger showed in his eyes and the firm set of his mouth. She should say something to him. Tell him it was going to be all right. Reassure him God was in control. But all she could do was gaze at him, stunned.

Someone had pictured her dead.

A startled gasp brought her gaze to the front of the desk. Mosey was gone, and Ginny had taken his spot. Mallory registered her friend's black fur coat and the pale green hat and scarf she'd knitted her for Christmas. Ginny could only see the picture upside down, but, judging from the horror covering her face, it was enough.

"Now this maniac is threatening your life? You've got to stop looking for this girl, Mallory." The words rushed out of Ginny even faster than usual. "What if the next card that comes in here has some poisonous substance in it instead of glitter and kills us all?"

"I've got to try to help her, Ginny. I promised." The words sounded lame to Mallory, but she didn't know how to lessen Ginny's fear without mentioning God, and Ginny didn't believe. "I can't stop searching."

"Then quit acting like you care about *us*. Stop asking us how we are, and acting friendly, and stop giving us presents. I don't want anything from you if you don't care enough to try to keep us safe!" Ginny yanked off her hat and tossed it at Mallory. It landed against her heart.

"Back off, Ginny," Shamus warned as he reached down and put his hand on Mallory's shoulder.

Emotions crashed in Mallory's head like waves on a seashore. Shamus was standing up for her. But that didn't mean he cared. It was just another way of protecting her.

"Oh, you," Ginny continued, turning her anger on Shamus, "you have no right to say anything. This is all your fault."

"Blame me all you want. Just don't take it out on Mallory."

"I don't want to take it out on anyone. I just don't want to be the target of some maniac again, either by mistake or on purpose."

Bess appeared in the doorway of her partitioned office, a phone pressed against her ear and her eyebrows raised to the ceiling. "You pipe down out here," she warned.

Mallory stared at Ginny, who avoided her gaze by looking at Bess. She had said "again" when she'd mentioned being a target. What had happened to her? It wasn't anything local, or she would have known about it, she was sure.

New York?

Bess monitored them as she concluded her phone conversation, pressed the hang-up button and turned to drop the phone back on her desk.

"That was a judge," she said, charging toward Mallory's desk, "and I could hardly hear him. What is going on out here that's more important than the work we're supposed to be doing?"

"I received a Christmas card from the bomber," Mallory told her. Amazing how calm she sounded, considering her hands were still shaking. Putting Ginny's hat down on one side of the desk, she pointed out the card on the other.

"I'll call the detective in charge of the case." Shamus went back to his desk and picked up his own phone, clearing the way for Bess to take his spot.

Her boss stared at the card. Her normal, all-business expression softened to worry as she focused on Mallory. "What does it say inside?"

"'Stop looking for Tara Tripp, or else.'" Ginny's voice was on edge. "Or else we all get murdered. Because she won't let the police handle looking for the kid. Shamus and Mallory need to work somewhere else until this maniac is caught."

"Ginny, you're not dead yet, and no one is going anywhere. Calm down," Bess said. "Better yet, go do some work. You, too, Renzo."

Mallory watched the two of them return to their desks. She had Bess's full attention now, and she really didn't want it. What she wanted was to crawl into bed and pull the covers over her head until the bomber was caught. He was threatening to kill her if she didn't stop looking for Tara. And maybe he wouldn't care if there were other casualties along the way.

But Tara was all alone. And she'd promised Bud Tripp. She couldn't go back on her word. She knew what that felt like when her brother had done it to her.

What was she supposed to do?

Shamus set the phone back in its cradle and motioned for Bess and Mallory to follow him to the hall, where they could talk in private. Once there, he closed the door to the office.

Through the window, Mallory watched as Tony went over to Ginny's desk, probably to console her.

Or maybe to plan Mallory's funeral.

Shamus spoke first. "My instincts tell me that card didn't come from the bomber, and Mallory isn't really in danger. It's a scare tactic."

"Explain," Bess ordered.

"Before the bomber blew up the probation building, he heard Mallory say that she would help Tara, no matter what. After that, we spotted a man disguised as Santa following Mallory. He was approaching the house she was in." He hesitated. "The—"

"Wait, don't tell me which house. I don't want to know," Bess said, sounding not at all happy. She waved her hand for him to go on. "Get to the point. We have probationers running amuck."

"The fake Santa ran when he saw me. Last night, we saw him again, and the same thing happened—he ran. So if the bomber has someone just watching or *following* her, but not actively trying to hurt her, it stands to reason he's thinking Mallory will lead him to Tara. For that he needs her alive."

Shamus's reasoning sounded logical to Mallory. "So who do you think sent the card?"

"It looks computer-generated to me. I'm guessing Tara herself, or a playmate with a nasty edge and some art talent who's helping her hide. They don't want you looking for her because they believe the bomber might be following you, and she's afraid."

So Shamus didn't think anyone was coming after her. That ought to make Ginny feel better. Mallory glanced back into the office, where her friend was gesturing wildly, probably planning her murder.

Or maybe not.

"The question is," Shamus asked, "what brought this on so suddenly?"

Both Bess and Shamus were looking at her. Mallory rubbed her mouth, not wanting to say, but she had no choice. A death threat was serious. "If Tara was in her old neighborhood, she might have seen me or found out I was there before work this morning looking for her. That's probably it, right?"

"Yeah, probably." Shamus merely shook his head at Mallory as if he wasn't at all surprised. She was afraid to look at Bess to see how she reacted. Shamus continued, "It could be Tara knows who the bomber is and that he wants to kill her to make sure she never turns him in. Otherwise, why worry about him finding her?"

The ball of dread in Mallory's stomach got bigger. "So if I lead him to Tara…"

"You're sentencing her to death. And if you get any time to talk to her, I think he'll kill you both, just to make sure she doesn't tell you who he is."

Bess didn't give Mallory time to think before turning to her. "I have a feeling even that isn't going to stop you from continuing to search for the girl. What I don't find out about, I can't be mad about. But if I see that you're not doing your work here, it's going to be your job."

At the top of the stairs they could hear voices, and Bess opened the office door, waving them back inside. As Mallory walked back to her desk, she saw Ginny and Mosey watching her, Ginny's face sullen, and Mosey's face sad.

It felt just like being home again.

At her desk, she found Ginny's scarf had joined her hat, an unspoken message. Mallory's bottom lip started to tremble. She and Ginny had been friends since Ginny had come back from New York. Years. Apparently no more.

She couldn't do any work until the police took the evidence off her desk, so she just sat in an empty chair between the desks and waited, praying silently for Ginny to understand why she wouldn't give up on Tara, wiping her teary eyes every few seconds.

Shamus hated seeing Mallory like this. In seconds, before she could stop him, he scooped up both the hat and scarf in his hands and was walking over to Ginny's desk.

"Here," he said, letting the scarf drift down in a soft green puddle on top of a file. "Don't strangle yourself with it."

"Shamus," Mallory said in a gently censuring tone.

Knowing that if he looked at her, she probably would tell him to let it be, and he would, he didn't. Instead, he plopped the hat on top of the scarf.

The door opened, and Detective Dickerson, who was working Tripp's murder, came through first, followed by Bess. When she saw Shamus by Ginny's desk, she raised her eyebrows, effectively barring him from saying anything else to Ginny. That was fine. He'd said all he was going to.

To Ginny. Mallory, though, was a different matter altogether. As soon as everyone cleared out of the office, he had a few things to say to her.

Five o'clock, closing time. After the long, hard day, Mallory was more than ready to leave and go to the tree decorating party at the Second Chance Assisted-Living Home.

She headed toward the coatrack and noticed Shamus's leather jacket was still hanging on it. Maybe she ought to find him and ask him to follow her home, but she didn't think it was necessary. After Dickerson had questioned her and cleared her desk, he'd told her that the danger to her outside was slight, as long as she didn't search for Tara.

She would again, but not tonight, so she'd be fine without Shamus.

If he was even planning to trail after her anymore. She

hadn't left the building again after the card had arrived, so she wasn't certain.

Taking her coat, Mallory turned from the rack and caught a glimpse of green beside Ginny's desk and took a sharp breath. Her scarf and hat were on top of the day's discarded papers, in the trash basket.

Don't get upset, she told herself. She had to think about Ginny. Her friend was really frightened for some reason. Even before the bombing, she'd seen signs of Ginny's fear— checking locked doors repeatedly, dwelling on crime in the news—but ignored them. But now the fear was taking the form of anger, at her.

As she bent and picked up the scarf set, hurt clamped down over her heart, and her chin quivered. She set it firmly in place. She couldn't let this get to her. Somehow, she needed to make peace with Ginny. She just hoped the Lord didn't need her to do it right away, because so help her, she couldn't.

"I'm sorry," Shamus said from about three feet inside the doorway. Too close for him not to have seen her pick up the items she held from Ginny's trash.

Drawing the side of her hand against her chin and lips, as though the act would wipe all telltale signs of being about to cry from her face, she turned and forced a smile she didn't feel. She had to let him see she could stand up under anything, and that he should, too. Nothing was impossible with God.

"Thanks," she said, wanting to cry all over again as she gazed back down at Ginny's scarf.

He frowned. "I meant about last night. I should have made it clear then that I'm not abandoning you. You shouldn't have gone to Tripp's old neighborhood without me."

"Absolutely." She bobbed her head in a nod. "You're right. And if you had been there, you could have kicked down the front door of Tripp's old house for me to see if Tara was hiding inside." Her smile no longer felt so forced. "As it was, I had to go away not knowing. I really needed you there this morning."

"I come in handy sometimes, don't I?" He grinned back, and some of the tension inside Mallory lightened. "But I'm here now. In fact, I plan on attending the decorating party at the Second Chance Home. What time does it begin?"

"Around seven," she told him happily. He might only be going to watch over her, but that didn't mean she couldn't try to get him together with Mr. Widemeyer.

"I'll follow you home now, and then I'll be back to follow you to Second Chance at a quarter till."

His gaze shifted to the scarf in her hands. "Ginny shouldn't have thrown it all away," he said in a low voice, so wistfully that Mallory wondered if he was referring to himself.

"She said she was afraid of being hurt again. I don't know what happened to her before, but I understand that kind of fear. It's a deep and gnawing dread that everything is going to explode suddenly. It never lets go until you eliminate the source." Mallory glanced at the scarf in her hands. "To Ginny, right now, I'm that source. She thinks if I stop fighting to find Tara, everything will be okay. She's wrong."

He didn't comment back, but his black velvet eyes told her he didn't agree. She didn't want to talk about Ginny anymore anyway. "I'm not sure—are you still singing in the cantata, or just attending to keep me safe?" she asked.

"I'm singing. I'm uncomfortable around Paul, but as you said, it will be a perfect gift for my mother. Besides, she already knows about it, and she's as hard for me to say 'forget it' to as you are."

Her breath caught. He was doing something he didn't want to do to keep her safe. She liked that.

"And I get to keep you safe from the bomber," he added. "That's important to me."

She noticed he hadn't said *she* was important to him, just that keeping her safe was.

Sighing, she stuffed Ginny's hat and scarf into her purse. After the kiss, she kept reading emotions and feelings into what he said, and she needed to stop doing that. She couldn't get all wrapped up in him. He was still the wrong type of man for her.

She had to stop thinking about that sort of thing.

"What are you going to do with the hat and scarf?" he asked as she zipped up her purse.

"Wash them and give them back to Ginny."

"You're going to forgive her for not standing up for you, are you?"

"I have to." She would, too. Just as soon as she calmed down.

"You have to because God wants us to forgive. Yeah, I know that. But that's just if the person who harmed you is sorry."

"Actually," she said as she slipped on her coat, "we can forgive them even if they aren't sorry. It's better to forgive, Shamus. You can keep things from eating away at you if you do."

"I'd believe you," he said quietly, "except I saw your face when Ginny threw the hat at you, and when you plucked the scarf out of the trash. It's eating at you plenty."

She wanted to deny that, but she couldn't. "You make me crazy, too, Shamus, and I'm not giving up on you."

He chuckled and reached for his jacket. "You're awfully good at that, you know. Not giving up on people. Me, Tara and Ginny. But how long can you keep fighting for us? How much are you willing to give up?"

"Whatever it takes." She meant that, too.

"Don't do that, Mallory. None of us is worth it. You are."

"And so are you, Shamus," she said, all her heart behind the words. "No matter what you think, you are."

He still looked doubtful, but it didn't matter. She was going to help Tara, find a way to make Ginny her friend again and, most of all, by Christmas, have Shamus be a changed man.

Even if she had to fight him all the way.

TEN

Mallory hadn't thought it possible. After only half an hour at the Second Chance Home, Shamus was having as much fun as she was.

"I just promised Mr. Widemeyer a chess game later," he said, handing her a cup of coffee in a throwaway cup he'd just braved the crowd for. "How soon will I be done here?"

He'd found Mr. Widemeyer himself. Now she wouldn't have to sneak away and contrive to throw the two of them together. The day was definitely improving.

"I can let you go in a minute. There are only a couple of ornaments left." Mallory gazed up at the eleven-foot-tall ever-green placed to one side of a set of sliding glass doors at the far end of the community room.

The tree had been decorated in shifts by the church-member volunteers, one shift putting up the twinkling lights, another the red, silver and green glass ornaments, and then she and Shamus the specially crocheted thread bells that she had worked on for the last year. He'd come in handy reaching the higher branches.

She looked back at Shamus, who stood admiring it as he polished off something like his fifth cookie.

"It looks nice now," he said, brushing his hands together to get rid of the crumbs and smiling again.

"It does. You are *really* enjoying yourself, aren't you?" she asked.

"It's the cookies. I'm in sugar shock." He gestured out into the recreation room that was filled with both residents and a large number of people from church who had shown up with a table full of sprinkled doughnuts, Christmas cookies and soda. "Blame them."

She grinned back at him and put her coffee down on a small table nearby, where she reached underneath into a medium-sized Christmas box for another ornament. As she rose, she caught a glimpse of a sprig of mistletoe in Shamus's hand. Slowly, deliberately, he raised it until he was holding it over his head.

It seemed such an out-of-character thing for him to do that she just stared at him for a minute, until she realized maybe it wasn't an out-of-character thing at all—for the *old* Shamus.

She kept staring at him, not knowing what to do. She couldn't kiss him. They were supposed to be *detaching*.

Maybe she should try those cookies he was having.

A squeal to her left made her tear her gaze away from him. "Look, girls, he's got mistletoe!" Four women, all near their eighties if they were a day, surrounded Shamus and took turns kissing his cheek, giggling like coeds scoping out a guy.

She burst into laughter herself and let the ladies have their fun. She hung the bell in her hand by its velvet-ribbon loop, and then the last one in the box, and by that time three of the women had floated away in search of their next victim. The fourth, the original squealer, looked at Mallory and shook her head.

"You better protect this guy better or one of us gals is going to scoop him up."

Mallory hid another smile. "I'll remember that."

The woman turned back to Shamus. "Sorry about that, but the men around here don't carry mistletoe."

Grinning, Shamus handed her his sprig. "Feel free to hang at will."

"Thank you!" The woman took the sprig and hurried off to her circle of friends, who were waiting a few feet away from her.

"I guess I got carried away with the spirit of the season," he told her.

"That will teach you to overindulge in sweets," she said, keeping a straight face somehow. "Face it, Shamus, you just can't handle those cookies anymore like you used to."

He laughed, and she started laughing right along with him. Their gazes locked. He wanted to kiss her again, she could tell. In public. Even though she knew it wasn't a good idea, every inch of her wanted to, every single inch. She closed her eyes as he started to tip his head, right there in the middle of everyone—

"Excuse me again!"

Her eyes bolting open, her cheeks blushing hot red with embarrassment, Mallory jumped apart from Shamus. The same elderly lady who'd called her girlfriends over was wiggling her fingers in front of them.

"I was so taken by the mistletoe, I forgot what I was coming over here for originally." She faced Shamus. "Someone said you were a police officer?"

"I was."

Shamus's eyes lost their sparkle and went all serious, and Mallory's heart fell. Not trouble, not now when he was just starting to be happy again.

"I thought you'd be the one to tell, then. I saw a figure outside the glass windows a couple of minutes ago. I don't know why anyone would be outside, just standing there by the window."

"I don't, either," Shamus said evenly, not alarming the woman in the least. If Mallory didn't know him so well, she would have thought he wasn't worried about a stranger out there. But she saw his hand brush against where his gun was holstered under his sweater as he moved to glance out the window. He was concerned.

He returned in seconds. "What did the man look like?"

"I don't know. That's just it. It's a bit darker out there than it is in here. I think he had a jacket on, and a hat pulled down around his ears. It was just so dark." She wrung her hands.

"Not a Santa suit?" Mallory asked.

"No, I would have noticed that, I think."

Mallory looked to see what Shamus thought, and he gave her a long look. If their stalker wasn't disguising himself now, could that mean the danger was escalating? She wanted to know, but couldn't ask in front of the mistletoe lady.

"You stay here," he said finally. "And I mean that." He left to work his way through the crowd in the large room.

"Shamus will find him if he's still out there, don't worry," Mallory reassured her. "Maybe it's just a church member who needed some air. Did you hang the mistletoe yet?"

She was changing the subject, but if the woman realized it, she apparently didn't mind. She reached into her sweater pocket and pulled out the green leaves and white berries.

"No, but I will," she said, smiling naughtily before she turned and rejoined her friends.

Mallory moved over to the sliding glass door and looked out the few feet she could see. Nothing appeared out of the ordinary. She couldn't help Shamus, so she went to where she'd left her coffee and began to sip it.

Shamus had wanted to kiss her again. The part of her that really wanted him to warred with plain good sense. Could she trust the change she was seeing in him? Would his reaching out to people continue beyond the party, or was he merely being nice here because they were elderly, and he'd be a recluse at work tomorrow? How did she really feel about him?

Too many questions, and absolutely no answers. Except for the very last one. She trusted him to keep her safe and to want what was best for her, and she was drawn to him. The connection she felt scared her, because what if she was wrong on the trust?

She couldn't bear to be hurt one more time.

She finished her coffee, got her Christmas box and brought it through the crowd to where she'd left her jacket hanging on the back of a chair, all the while looking to see if Shamus had returned.

That's when she saw Luke Cramer approaching. He still wore his jacket, and her eyes narrowed when she felt the cold from outside drifting around him. He'd just come inside. Could Luke have been the man outside the window?

"You're frowning." Luke's gray-blue eyes slanted at her. "Aren't you happy to see me?"

She didn't want to lie, but the truth was, she probably wouldn't have given Luke a second thought if he hadn't found her in the crowd. Shamus, on the other hand...

"I'm sorry." She was. He didn't deserve to be treated like that. She didn't want to hurt Luke's feelings, so she went on tiptoe and gave him a quick kiss on the cheek. "It's been a really bad day." Until Shamus had told her he was coming to the party.

"That's too bad," he said, his voice filled with so much sympathy she gave him a small smile. "What happened?"

"Disasters in every corner. But hopefully, they're over." *Please, Lord, let them be over, and Shamus be all right.*

"Yeah," Luke said, agreeing. "My day was perfect. Just finished dinner with a client and landed a big account." Luke worked in his family-owned insurance company. "It made me late getting here, but it means more money in the bank. That's the important thing."

Was it? She gazed at the crowd of people who were all

talking and laughing with the home's residents, quite a few of whom didn't have any family left. She would bet they thought there were more important things than money.

He unzipped his jacket and glanced at the refreshment table. "I'm getting some coffee, and then we'll see if I can't make your day even better."

His words shouldn't have made her nervous, but they did. He splashed some coffee in a cup and returned as if running a dash.

"Any work left to do on the decorating?" he asked. She wondered if his coffee had peppermint in it, because she was smelling that.

"The tree's done." She lifted her sleeve and glanced at the large face of her Santa-face watch. Eight o'clock. She shifted her gaze from Luke to the front door, but no one was coming or going.

Where was Shamus? Was he all right?

"Good. Then I can have your full attention?"

She stared up at Luke, wondering what he'd say if she asked him to go outside with her to check on Shamus. She already knew what Shamus would say.

But if he were in trouble, what would it matter?

"I can, can't I?"

She shot her gaze back at him. "Can what?"

"Have your full attention?"

She glanced one more time toward the front door, and took in Shamus's former father-in-law talking to the group of ladies with the mistletoe and would have kept watching to see if they swooped down on him with kisses, except Luke moved so that he blocked her gaze.

"Your attention?"

Was it her imagination, or did he sound annoyed? He was smiling, so it was hard to tell.

"I'm sorry," she said, giving him an edgy smile. "I have a lot on my mind."

"How about if we go someplace more private?"

"I know just the place." Private, but not too private. Shamus had warned her not to go anywhere alone with Luke, and besides, she wanted to be out here when Shamus returned.

"Anywhere without people," Luke said, reaching for her jacket. She put her hand on his arm.

"I was thinking more like down by the library." At his confused look, she added, "They have one here. We had a tour of the building last year. I'll show you."

Ignoring the disappointment in Luke's eyes as he dropped her jacket on the chair seat, she threaded her way through small groups of people, trusting him to follow. Halfway to the hallway, Shamus's former father-in-law flagged her down with a wave of two fingers.

"Where did Shamus disappear to, do you know?" he asked.

Luke gave an impatient sigh behind her. She couldn't help it; she couldn't be rude to Shamus's former in-law. "He's outside. He should be back in shortly."

She hoped. She continued on until she got to a short hall. She stopped just a little way down it, her heart beating hard. Why? she wondered. It wasn't like she was somewhere alone with Luke. People were going back and forth past the mouth of the hall, just a few feet away.

It was probably just nerves from the death threat earlier today. But Luke wouldn't have any reason to kill her, or to be after…

Startled, she remembered when Shamus and Luke had come face-to-face, and the antagonism she'd felt between the two. Shamus had told her to watch herself around Luke, but surely if he suspected Luke of being the bomber, he would have clued her in.

"At last," Luke said. "Maybe this will help cheer you up.

I got your Christmas present." He reached into his open jacket and pulled out a small rectangular gift, impeccably wrapped in shiny green. "Open it."

This was just not her day. A teddy bear dressed like Santa or a box of candy would have been one thing. But Luke's present looked suspiciously like *jewelry*. He had big-ticket tastes, so it would probably be expensive jewelry. If she was right, she'd have to turn down the gift.

"Go ahead, open it."

She took the package, which was very light. No sense in second-guessing him. Maybe there were movie tickets inside. "I didn't get you a present."

Disappointment shaded his face. "Just open it."

His words sounded like an order, and she frowned at him.

"Sorry," he said, giving her a sheepish grin. "It's just that our friendship means a lot to me, and I've been waiting since the last practice to give this to you. You always give nice things to people, and I wanted to be someone who gives really nice things to you."

She remembered how she'd felt when she thought Shamus wasn't going to accept her present. Terrible. She couldn't do that to anyone.

Carefully lifting the parts that were taped down, she unfolded the paper to reveal a velvet-covered box. Tierney's, the most expensive jeweler in the city.

She opened it. It was a gold chain with a heart made up of little gems that looked suspiciously like—

"Like it?" Luke asked. "They're diamonds. Prettiest necklace I could find. I thought it would make you see how I feel about you." He got closer and leaned down, as if he was going to kiss her. But she couldn't, not when she kept thinking about Shamus and wanting to kiss *him*.

"Luke, I can't accept this." She backed up to avoid him, and hit the wall. She edged sideways, hoping to just go to the end of the hall, rejoin the party and avoid a scene, but Luke's arms went either side of her as he braced himself against the wall.

"It's okay. We're dating," Luke said. "And hopefully more. Of course you can accept it."

She was pinned in, and she started breathing hard, fear hitting her in the gut. What to do? She didn't want to make a scene and ruin the party for everyone.

"Luke, you should—"

"Kiss you?" he interrupted. "Yes." He leaned forward. The box dropped from her fingers, and she pushed up his forearms and stepped on his foot as hard as she could, considering the angle. Instead of having the hoped-for result—Luke hopping away in pain—he grabbed her arms and pinned them against the wall.

"You shouldn't have done that," he said.

She twisted and yanked, but his face came nearer, as if she posed a challenge. She'd let him get too far.

She sensed a big shadow to her left, and then Luke went flying away from her as if he'd suddenly sprouted wings. She pulled in a long breath and let the wall support her as she watched Shamus twist Luke's arm and shove him against the opposite wall, face-first.

"See how it feels?" Shamus's voice was threatening and filled with fury. "Stay away from her, Cramer, or I'll personally make sure you don't touch anyone ever again."

"Let go of me," Luke told him, his tone defiant. Mallory saw him catch sight of the people at the end of the hall. "I didn't do anything to her. We've been dating for a year, and she just gave me the wrong signal."

She felt her cheeks flood with heat, and glanced to the women at the end of the hall, some of them church members. "I did not," she said simply. Any more protest than that might seem like she was protesting too much. Luke was very respected at church, and from what he'd told her, he tithed big money. With some people, that would hold a lot of weight when it came to who believed whom.

Shamus thumped him against the wall again. "You want him locked up for assault, Mallory?" he asked over his shoulder. "I can arrange it."

She glanced at the onlookers at the end of the hall, and then at her shaking hands. She didn't want to go through a court appearance. She wasn't even sure a judge would believe assault.

"No, Shamus, let him go. Please."

Shamus backed off to stand protectively in front of her. He kicked the jewelry toward Luke, who scooped it up and took off wordlessly down the hall. When he was gone, Shamus turned to her.

Without asking her if she was all right, he picked up her wrists and looked at the angry red marks there, his eyes grim. He didn't even say a word, for which she was grateful. If he made one remark about what had just happened, she would start crying.

"I didn't find anything outside," he said, slipping his arm around her shoulders and walking with her down the hallway. The ladies at the end dispersed, but not before Mallory noticed a disapproving frown or two. An open hall hardly qualified as a clandestine meeting, but she had a feeling that by tomorrow, that's exactly what it would be called in the gossip circles.

"Luke came in a couple minutes after you went out to look," she told him, glad he was close. "He said he had a late dinner. Could he have been watching us?"

"I don't think bombing is his M.O. He's more the type to hurt women."

She met his eyes. "He tried something with Ruth?" she said softly, since they were very near people now.

"Yeah. When he touched Ruth, that was the first time I warned him." Shamus didn't attempt to lower his voice. He didn't really care who heard. Luke Cramer was a menace to women and ought to be out of the church. "Today was the second. He'd better be more careful, because three strikes and he's out."

"Hearing that, I'm glad I stepped on his foot as hard as I could," she said.

"You did?" Shamus almost smiled, but he was still too angry.

"It didn't do any good at all."

"He probably was wearing steel-toed shoes. I imagine his feet get stepped on a lot when he's around women."

Her lips almost twisted upward. Shamus was glad. She was trembling again, and making jokes was all he dared do here to comfort her. Someone had definitely been watching them outside.

He could see people leaning their heads together, whispering, and knew the news was traveling fast. He saw the frowns directed at him.

He needed to get out of here. A quick survey of the room, which had thinned out some, told him Cramer had left.

And that Mr. Widemeyer was waiting patiently for him by a small table that held a chess set.

Oh, man.

"You're still on the cleanup committee?" he asked her. That meant she'd be at least another hour.

Mallory nodded, continuing toward where her jacket sat. Shamus gently touched her shoulder to get her to stop.

"I think it might be easier on you if I left," he told her quietly. He had a feeling the women of the church would then offer her the comfort he dared not. He glanced at his watch. "I'll be back at nine-thirty to follow you home."

"Okay," she said, her deep green eyes gazing up at him. They widened and her fingers fluttered toward his neck.

"Where's your scarf?" she asked.

"I don't know." He'd worn it this evening, and won another soft smile from Mallory. "Maybe somebody picked it up to admire it and forgot to put it back."

At least, he thought as he went toward Mr. Widemeyer to explain why he had to leave now, that's what he hoped had happened to it. But he had a bad feeling about its disappearance.

He glanced toward where he'd left Mallory standing, and already two women were talking to her. One was even patting her shoulder. He desperately wanted to shepherd her right out of this party and hold her in his arms. Had one elderly lady not seen someone watching them, he would have.

Could that someone watching have been Luke Cramer? He should find him and ask. While he was at it, maybe he should put the fear of God in the man and haul him down to the police station with a citizen's arrest for assaulting Mallory. He didn't know if it would stick, but it would be really satisfying to see Cramer's fear.

Where was Shamus? The next morning, Mallory said another prayer that everything was all right with him as she locked her car and hurried into the courthouse. He'd promised last night, when he'd followed her home from the Second Chance, that he would return in the morning to follow her to work. The man watching them through the sliding doors had made them both nervous.

But Shamus hadn't shown up this morning and hadn't answered his cell. Something was wrong. She knew it. Shamus wasn't the type to break promises.

Lord, please let him be in the office. Please?

She hurried inside and stopped short at the sight of Shamus's empty desk. No jacket on the rack, either.

"You're here," Mosey said, surprise in his eyes. He sat at his desk, leaning back, hands behind his head.

"Where else would I be?" she asked, her heart thudding.

"At the police station, bailing Shamus out."

If Mosey had just hit her with a brick on the head, she couldn't have been more stunned.

The older man noticed. "You didn't hear? According to gossip, the police charged him with beating a guy unconscious somewhere between eight-thirty and nine-thirty last night. It was all over the courthouse this morning. They say he set the Christmas tree in the town square on fire, too."

Shamus? What fire? Mallory took a couple of steps backward, shaking her head hard in denial. "Shamus would never set a tree on fire. He just wouldn't. What would be the point?"

"He hated Christmas," Mosey said. "We all saw that. Maybe he was making a statement."

This had to be the bomber's work. She was disappointed in Mosey. "Surely you know better than that. He couldn't do any of it."

"Anyone is capable of beating someone unconscious," he said. "Take it from me. Especially your buddy."

"Sure he is," she said. "But only if it was self-defense, and then only if he had to. And then, Mosey, he would stick around and call the police himself. Arresting him for this is just ridiculous."

"Is it?" Mosey said. "They found the scarf you knitted for him there."

Which didn't bother her at all. "He was set up. The scarf disappeared last night at the nursing home we were decorating."

Mosey's hands dropped from behind his head, and he sat up straight. For the first time since she'd met him, Mosey looked irritated with her. She sucked in her breath and tried to pretend she hadn't just lost one more friend. "Who was the victim?" she asked. "One of his former arrests?"

"I don't know," Mosey said.

"It was Luke Cramer," Mallory heard from behind her. "And he's in a coma."

She switched her gaze to Ginny, who stood in the doorway with an apologetic look in her eyes. The blonde came inside, put her purse down on her desk and hung up her coat without a single disparaging remark about what Shamus was accused of doing. "Can we talk?"

Mallory hesitated. Something had changed with Ginny, but finding out what would delay her getting to Shamus.

"I have to bail Shamus out. Please tell Bess that."

Instead of looking hurt, Ginny merely nodded and sat down at her desk.

The police station was only on the next block, so Mallory walked. Fast. A couple of times she broke into a run, almost slipping on ice. She didn't care. Shamus's getting arrested wasn't right. It just wasn't right. He would not hurt Luke Cramer that badly and then leave.

Flashing her probation officer's badge at the front desk, she found out where Shamus was and prayed all the way up the stairs. Prayed that she wouldn't lose her temper. Because every nerve in her felt like a time bomb waiting to go off.

She shuddered at the very thought.

Pushing through the heavy door, she spotted Shamus and immediately began to feel calmer. He wasn't behind bars, at least not yet. There was still time to talk reason to the arresting cop. The man's back was mostly to her, until he turned his gaze from the computer screen in front of him toward Shamus to say something to him and she caught his full features from the side.

Detective Dickerson. Her heart plummeted. She did not like

Dickerson. The entire time he'd questioned her about the card, she'd felt guilty of something, but she didn't even know what.

Lord, I'm going to need big help with this one.

Taking a deep breath, she strode toward the two and started talking the second she got close enough.

"How could Shamus be under arrest? He didn't hurt Luke Cramer, and he certainly didn't burn down a Christmas tree."

There. She hadn't accused Dickerson of not knowing his job or any of the other noncharitable things she was thinking about him.

Dickerson scowled at her. "Someone at your party last night phoned in a tip that Shamus had fought with Cramer and left shortly after him. I just brought him in for questioning. He's not under arrest." He paused. "Who told you he was under arrest?"

"A coworker." She gazed down at Shamus and mouthed Mosey's name.

"Figures," Shamus said. "Hope the rumor doesn't make it to my family." His face held the same expression it had right after he'd tackled Tripp in his mother's yard and thought Tripp might have planted a bomb.

"If you're not arrested, then I can't bail you out, take custody of you and drag you to whatever church function I like," Mallory said, because she hated seeing him all intense like this again. "I was really looking forward to that."

His eyes softened perceptibly. He wanted to grin at her. He might even have done so, had not Dickerson said, "That's not to say I won't arrest him."

Not only did Shamus scowl, but anger flooded back into her. She took a deep breath. Control. She could not be like her father.

Lord, I need more help here.

But it was too late to control her escalating anger. "You can't seriously be thinking about arresting him." Her voice rose with every word. "If Shamus beat up someone as badly as I hear happened, he'd have wounds on him somewhere. Especially fighting someone as big as Luke Cramer. And I saw him at nine-thirty, and he looked fine, wearing the same clothes—"

Dickerson held up his hand. "You'll get your turn. For now—"

The phone on the desk rang, and Dickerson yanked it up.

She met Shamus's eyes. Much as his being angry upset her, a small part of her was also glad. At least he was reacting to the injustice of being hauled in for questioning instead of going into that shell of not caring.

"He says he's what?" Dickerson said, his voice rising. "Yeah, send him up." Hanging up the phone, he swiveled back to face both of them.

"Well, isn't this something. There's a guy down there who says he's been following you."

"Who?" Shamus asked.

"Santa Claus."

ELEVEN

"Oh, boy. Am I ready to meet *him*." Mallory yanked her purse's shoulder strap up higher. "Shamus, where's your Glock?"

Dickerson's frown deepened as he pushed his chair back and sized her up for her threat level.

"Mallory," Shamus said quietly, "I'd like to get out of here sometime today. Tell the nice detective that's just your irritation talking, and you really are gentle and reserved."

"I don't know what I am anymore," she told him, folding her arms over her chest. "Because of this guy, I've lived with constant anxiety over the past few days. It wouldn't bother me if he was threatened a little, too."

"So here's your chance." Dickerson waved his fingers behind them. "But watch the violence level."

Mallory turned to look. Santa had pushed through the main door. A couple of detectives at the far right of the huge office laughed and called out a "Hello, Santa!" to him, and she could hear giggles as more people sighted him.

The fake Santa didn't pay any attention to them. Stopping a few feet away, he pulled off his beard and two strips of snowy-white eyebrows, revealing a face that was startlingly familiar to Mallory.

She moved sideways to sink onto the chair Shamus had vacated, biting into her bottom lip.

"Mallory?" Shamus took her hand and squeezed it gently. "Who is he?"

"Ethan." More filled out and more powerful-looking than he'd been when she'd last seen him at eighteen, but it was her brother. She'd stared at his picture enough times to remember.

Santa's headgear in his hand, Ethan came close enough to talk and regarded Shamus with an assessing look.

But Shamus was not the one he had to fear, Mallory thought as she narrowed her eyes. "You've been following me," she said. "Why?"

"Because I promised you once if you needed me, I would be there for you. When I heard about the bombing, I came to protect you."

"I needed you years ago. Where were you then?"

Ethan took a deep breath. "I can't explain that to you right now, Mallory, but believe me, I knew you'd be all right if I left town."

"Why didn't you just tell me it was you?"

"I thought you'd be angry and make me leave."

She would have.

"The important thing is that I'm here now, for your friend." Ethan turned to Dickerson. "Burke didn't hurt anyone."

Mallory was torn between wanting to hug Ethan and wanting to run out of there and never see him again. She would have started yelling at him for leaving her behind, but if he knew something that would get Shamus out of this mess, she needed to hear it.

"And who are you, exactly?" Detective Dickerson asked Ethan. "Another boyfriend of hers?" He flicked his finger at Mallory.

"Dickerson, be very careful," Shamus said. "I'm not real happy right now."

Ethan waited until Dickerson had finished scowling at Shamus. "My name is Ethan Larsen. I'm Mallory's brother."

Dickerson's gaze moved from him to Mallory and back again. "You were following your sister, and you didn't tell her?"

"I had my reasons."

Dickerson rolled his eyes upward, as if asking for help from God. For the first time, Mallory felt a twinge of sympathy for the detective.

"So what's with the dressing as Santa?" Dickerson asked.

"It's Christmas," Ethan said.

"I'm not impressed with that answer," Dickerson told him. Mallory wasn't either.

"I've been gone a long time—"

"Years," Mallory broke in. Bitterly, but she couldn't help it. She was furious with Ethan, and all the Christmas spirit in the world wasn't going to fix that.

Her brother worked his jaw from side to side. "I have my reasons for not wanting anyone to know I was back in Shepherd Falls, Detective. In fact, I wouldn't have returned, except I heard about the bombing and came here to try to protect Mallory."

And didn't that beat all? Exasperation joined all the other emotions Mallory was feeling. "I don't understand, Ethan. I prayed for you to come back for years. Why wouldn't you want me to know you were here?"

"Right now is not the time for a reunion," Ethan told her bluntly. Maybe even rudely. Mallory wanted to kick him, but they weren't kids anymore.

"We need to get Burke out of here," he continued. "You want my help, or not?"

She didn't. That would mean she'd owe him, and just like

with Shamus, she didn't want to owe her brother anything. Ethan didn't care about her, or he would have stuck around.

But she was desperate to help Shamus, so she pursed her lips and folded her arms across her chest. Some grown-up she was being, but then again, Ethan had been the one dressing up in a Santa costume.

She glanced at Shamus for support. He was trying very hard not to smile. Great.

"Would you just get on with it?" Dickerson asked Ethan.

Her brother nodded. "I've been following Mallory with the idea of watching where she went and making sure another bomb wasn't planted in a building with her inside. I was in the parking lot at the nursing home last night where the two of them were." He tilted his chin toward her and Shamus. "About eight-thirty, I saw Burke come out of the building. He sat in his car for an hour, at which time he went back inside the building. A few minutes later, he came out again with Mallory. They went to her apartment complex and talked in the parking lot for almost fifteen minutes."

"You sat there watching us?" Mallory asked, thanking the Lord above Shamus hadn't kissed her again. She didn't want her brother knowing how much she liked Shamus. *She* was none of Ethan's business, no matter what her brother thought.

"I was watching out for you," Ethan clarified.

She almost asked him what the difference was, but he continued on with what he had witnessed.

"Mallory went inside her apartment, Burke left and I left. When I passed the town square, the fire trucks were already there. There's no way Burke went near that guy who got hurt."

"Before I came outside and sat in my car, what else did you see?" Shamus asked.

Dickerson made a noise in his throat and threw a warning glance at him. For interfering in his questioning, Mallory supposed. Shamus didn't react. Apparently he was used to Dickerson. Or he didn't care what Dickerson thought. Yeah. With Shamus, the latter was more likely.

"One man rushed out before you did," Ethan told him. "Short blond hair, tall, no hat or scarf. Could have been a linebacker."

"That would have been Luke," Mallory broke in. "He told me he *was* a linebacker in college. Big and quick. I don't understand. Why couldn't he defend himself better?"

"Kind of hard to do when you've been drinking and smacked in the head from behind with a blunt object," Dickerson said.

He'd been drinking? That could explain the way he'd acted with her. If he'd drank more after he'd left the decorating party, he'd have been an easy victim.

Putting someone in a coma and then phoning in a tip hoping Shamus might take the fall for his assault—or for his death, if Luke didn't recover. Had the bomber hoped Luke would die and Shamus would be imprisoned for *murder?*

What else would the man be willing to do?

"Did you see anyone else go in or out?" Shamus asked.

"Shortly after the linebacker, another man came outside. I couldn't tell much about him because he had a hat and scarf on. Dark leather jacket. He walked to a van parked on the street, spoke through the open window for a minute, then went back inside."

She saw Shamus's eyes narrow. "Was he wearing the scarf when he came back in?"

Ethan ran his hand through his wavy chestnut hair in frustration. Mallory remembered him doing that when they were kids.

"Sorry," he said finally. "I don't recall."

"Shamus didn't have his scarf when he left the nursing home around eight-thirty, Detective," Mallory broke in. "I specifically noticed it. We figured someone must have taken it."

All three of them looked at Dickerson expectantly.

The man whooshed out a breath from the side of his mouth. "I'm letting you go, Burke, since the two of them are giving you an alibi, and I can believe they didn't prepare it beforehand." Dickerson waved his hand through the air. "Mr. Larsen, can you stick around and give me a formal statement?"

"Yes. Just give me a couple minutes." Ethan turned to Mallory.

"I'm not talking to you," she said before he could ask. Now Shamus would probably think her petty, but right then, that was the way things had to be.

Turning, she headed off toward the door. She could sense the two men following her, and rather than risk another scene in the middle of the police station—her storming in earlier was enough for one day—she stopped and faced them.

"What do you want out of me, Ethan? I can't create feelings for you I don't have."

"Can we meet for lunch? It's important. I have to explain something to you."

"She'll be there," Shamus said for her.

"Oh, no, Shamus," Mallory said, gripping her purse strap. "Letting you speak for me is so not on my agenda for you."

She moved her slanted-eyed gaze to her brother. "And you. I'm not interested, Ethan. If you had anything to say to me, you should have come back years ago."

"Fine," Shamus broke in again. He pulled a business card out of his pocket to give to Ethan. "I'll meet you for lunch."

Hurt jolted through her. She'd run over here, scared to death for Shamus, believing in his innocence despite what Mosey had implied, and the least he could do is pretend her brother didn't exist like she wanted to.

"I have things to ask him."

She couldn't turn Shamus down, not for anything. With a

small humph of breath, she turned to Ethan. "Don't think for one minute I'm doing this for you." She glanced back for a second at Shamus, who gave her a shadow of a smile. "The Steel Diner, at twelve-fifteen. And don't wear your Santa outfit. You look like a buffoon."

She yanked open the heavy steel door and left them behind.

"I didn't think I looked that bad," Ethan said, glancing down at what was left of his Santa costume.

"That's just the sister in her coming out, whether she wants it to or not."

Ethan looked bemused.

"I'd better go after her," Shamus told him.

"Wait. I'm asking you to make sure Mallory doesn't go after Tara Tripp. No matter what she hears, or what she finds out. It could mean Tara's life." With that, Ethan took off toward Dickerson.

Shamus scowled after him. Tara's life? He was only worried about Mallory's. That aside, Ethan had just made it obvious there was something else going on with Tara. He didn't want to question him in front of the detective, so he opened the door to go find Mallory.

He found her waiting for him next to the nearby exit, still safely inside the police building. When she spotted him, she flashed him a soft smile, one he hadn't seen much in the last two days and missed a lot.

He mentally shook himself. He'd gotten too used to her smiles. He needed to stop watching for them. Stop hoping for them. Stop living for them.

"Even though I don't want to talk to Ethan," she said as they went outside and headed toward the courthouse, dodging melting slush piles, "I guess I owe him for showing up to help you."

"Aren't you curious as to what he wants to talk to you about?"

Her long curls flip-flopped as she shook her head. "I told

you. Ethan broke his promise and left years ago. He never bothered to check up on me. Not so much as a call. I'm not inclined to care about anything he has to say."

"You care about everyone. You even care about Ginny, who just did worse to you than your brother did."

"No, she didn't. There's nothing worse than abandoning someone," she said flatly. "Nothing."

His eyes grew wide as her statement hit him in the gut.

She stopped short in the middle of the sidewalk and grab his arms.

"Shamus, I didn't mean you," she said. "I wasn't even thinking about you when I said that. You didn't abandon your wife. You were just late to pick her up."

"Yeah. Too late," he said grimly. He should have known better than to enjoy Mallory's smile, even for just a minute.

"I'm sorry," she said, her eyes teary. "I think the world of you. I would never hurt you."

"Yeah, I know." She'd come running to save him from Dickerson when there hadn't been a thing she could do. She really did care.

He took her arm and started walking again down the busy city street. God just kept reminding him of how he'd failed Ruth. He wasn't going to fail Mallory. He would keep her safe until the police caught the bomber, or he would die. Assuming he survived, then he would think about finding a new job. He didn't want to fall for her any deeper than he already had, not with a possible line of maniacs waiting to get out of prison and hurt her to get to him. And he couldn't ask her to live with that over her head. He'd never see her smile again.

Any chance of his happiness was over, but he could save hers.

"Ethan warned that you shouldn't try to find Tara. I got the impression he knows something we don't."

His voice sounded guarded again. Mallory hated herself.

She always used to watch what she said to make sure she didn't hurt people, because her father never had, and he'd hurt her so badly. All it had taken to become like Gideon Larsen was being unraveled.

Just as he had been.

"What more could Ethan know?" she asked Shamus. "The bomber kidnapped Tara to get her father to cooperate and bomb the office, and it's related to you somehow, probably revenge. She escaped, and now the guy is after her because she can identify him. There isn't anything more to it."

"He seemed positive. I hope we find out at lunch. But until then, promise me you won't sneak off to look for Tara?"

"Sure. I can promise noon. While I wait, I'll actually get some work done."

"Bess will be so pleased," Shamus said. But he didn't smile, so she didn't, either.

Shamus's cell rang when they were almost to the top of the courthouse steps. He took it out and checked the number as they continued inside the courthouse lobby, where he headed away from the door.

"I need to take this." With a quick glance at her, Shamus excused himself and moved far enough away that she couldn't hear the conversation. She could, however, see the hurt in his eyes as he spoke with the caller.

She couldn't stand to see Shamus looking that way.

Finally he hung up without a goodbye and pocketed his phone. She hurried over to him. "What's wrong, and what can I do to fix it?"

His face was once again wearing a mask of indifference. "I guess Mom's going to have to be disappointed. That was Paul McCauley."

His former father-in-law certainly had the ability to hurt Shamus's feelings, thought Mallory.

"Since he knows me well, he volunteered to call. Thought the news might be a little easier to take, coming from him. Apparently people are upset at the church. I've been asked not to attend church or anything to do with the cantata until whoever's creating this havoc is arrested. They're afraid one of them could be attacked next if I'm around."

Oh, no. "I cannot believe this is happening." She shook her head slowly. "I'll talk to the elders. And the people in the cantata. Everyone. I'll tell them it's not your fault—"

"Don't do that, Mallory. You don't need them turning against you, too. Just accept it. This is how people really are."

She started to protest.

"Think about it," he said quietly. "The people in the office, the ones at church—even your brother. They all do what seems right to them. They look out for themselves. It's human nature. You should never put your trust in anyone." He turned to continue on to the office.

She caught up to him. "I trust you, Shamus."

He halted his steps, turned to her and shot her one of the intense stares she didn't like to see.

"Don't," he said quietly. "Please don't trust me. I'm here for you now, but I'll only make you unhappy in the long run. I'll never be the man I once was. The person you want back again."

He could, she wanted to protest. But his eyes were warning her against it.

"We'd better get downstairs before Bess sends out the police," he told her.

He was trying to joke. She wouldn't have believed the phone call had affected him in the least—if she hadn't seen his eyes when he was talking to Paul.

"I'm getting something to drink before I go downstairs." Something without caffeine. She was tense enough. He shrugged and left her behind, and she continued to the snack room.

"Am I getting this all wrong, God?" she asked under her breath, shoving quarters in the soda machine and punching the button for a bottle of cold water flavored with lemon. "Am I a fool?"

No answer came to her as she sat at one of the tables in the empty room, twisted the lid and started drinking.

Was Shamus right? Was he too embittered now to ever find joy in life again? She didn't know. All she did know was she wanted to help Shamus and save a teenager, and she wasn't doing either.

In fact, she'd done some damage. He'd been perfectly content, in a sad way, being disconnected from people before. She'd made him get involved to the point he was enjoying life, and now things were worse than ever for him.

As she recycled her bottle and got ready to go back to work, she prayed, asking God to help Shamus to be happy again. After seeing the glimpses of the man he could be, she wanted that so much for him.

And for her. Her feelings for Shamus ran so deep she was awfully afraid they might even be the beginning of love. She couldn't be in love with the man she'd just seen, cynical and covering up his feelings, but maybe she could with the man who'd helped her decorate the tree, and brought cookies to her to help get her through bad news, and who'd stood up for her and saved her life….

The real Shamus underneath the guilt.

Shamus's only real hope of a life was for them to catch the bomber. Through Tara Tripp. Even her brother seemed to think the teenager was important. To find her, it was time to stop being so accommodating and polite to Tara's friends.

No, it was time to stop being so nice and sweet to *everyone*, and start fighting to get what she wanted.

Shamus, happy.

* * *

They sat at the Steel Diner for over thirty minutes, and Ethan didn't show. Shamus was puzzled, but Mallory wasn't surprised. She hadn't expected otherwise. She'd used the time to talk to him about putting pressure on Keisha and Alexis to find Tara.

They were still arguing when they exited his car and headed back to work. Or rather, Shamus was.

"After thinking about it, I'll admit your idea of trying to smoke the bomber out using Tara might be sound," Shamus told her. "*If* I could believe she's actually in danger. She could be working with the bomber, for all we know."

They crossed Lot 1 onto the sidewalk that led to the front of the courthouse. "If she is, then why would she tell me he would kill her if he found her?"

His arched eyebrow said she should know the answer to that.

"Okay, people lie. But I heard Tara's voice. She was scared, Shamus." Her chin lifted stubbornly as she glanced at him. "You're just in a bad mood because my brother lied to you and didn't show up."

"You knew he wouldn't."

"Almost. I *figured* he wouldn't. That's just a shade short of knowing." She stuck her hands in her pockets as they reached the wide, circular steps in front of the courthouse entrance and started the climb upward.

At the top, slightly winded from her fast climb, she stopped, pulled in a breath of the chilly air and faced the tall man at her side.

"My guess is, just like before, Ethan decided to go his own way again. On the bright side, hey, maybe this time he'll send me a letter. But I'm not counting on it."

Her eyes were getting moist. She took her hand out of her pocket and wiped at their corners. They were not tears. She was *not* crying because her brother didn't care. She didn't care about him, either, so tears over him would be stupid.

"Something might have happened to him, Mallory," Shamus said. "I'll call Sullivan and see what he can find out."

"You're wasting your time."

"It's my time. Ethan's disappearance is worrying me. On the other subject, since I really don't want you going off alone on this, I'll work on finding Tara Tripp."

She gaped at him, heedless of the people who were passing by them on the steps. "You're changing your mind about fighting?"

"Yeah." He paused. "I can't go on like this. I need this guy to stop. And you're right. Finding Tara might just be the fastest way to find the bomber. Maybe even the only way."

"I think I love you!" she said, flinging her arms around him right there, happiness flooding her, pushing away her anger at everything that had happened that morning. Shamus would help her with Tara, the teenager would be safe and her promise to Bud Tripp would be filled.

Even better than that, Shamus was going to fight for his future, and he was hugging her back.

Shockwaves reverberated through both of them, and Mallory's knees went weak. It took her a couple of seconds to realize what she had felt wasn't her love for him rushing through her.

It was a bomb.

She stepped backward from Shamus, her gaze flying toward the source of the sound in the parking lot they'd just left. Two lots behind where Shamus had found a parking space, debris fell around what was left of *her* SUV and the fireball that was burning in it.

The bomber.

She bolted toward the relative safety of the building.

Shamus followed. The guard who manned the metal detector was already heading toward them. Jacob. His name was Jacob. She opened her mouth to warn him, but she couldn't speak.

"Bomb exploded in the parking lot," Shamus said.

The guard nodded and pulled out a cell phone, continuing outside to take a look. Shamus pulled her to a spot away from the door and then stepped far enough away from her to check her for damage.

"You're okay," he declared, his eyes filled with concern.

"No, I am definitely *not* okay." She began to pace. "There was a blanket in the back of my SUV that I've been knitting during my breaks and lunch hour for the better part of a year. It was almost done. It was going to be for my mother, and *he* wrecked it. Do you have any idea how much my mother looked forward to that blanket? She's been badgering me for years to make her one, and now I'll have to tell her some maniac blew it up, and then she'll want me to move home again, and if I do, I'll lose what I've worked so hard for, I'll become bitter and unhappy."

She stopped pacing and drew a deep breath. "That's it. I already thought it this morning, but now I'm positive. I'm done. No more Mister Nice Guy. This idiot is stepping all over me. It's war."

Hearing chuckling, she finally focused in on Shamus "Why are you laughing?"

Shamus grinned at her, even as his gaze swept the quickly filling lobby they were in. "Because you're funny when you're not being nice."

"You're right. That wasn't nice, it was mean-spirited, and it's not Christian behavior." She remembered Shamus's hurt when she'd forgotten herself that morning. She found a nearby chair along the wall and sank into it, feeling guilty now.

"I'm sorry," she said more softly. "I've been through an emotional wringer today. Maybe I should go home and start again."

"You have a right to be angry, Mallory. Some people deserve your anger."

Her father. Ethan. And definitely the bomber. She met Shamus's eyes again. They were focused on her, tentative, gentle. The grin had left his handsome face, and he was gazing at her as if he cared about her—no, more than cared. Maybe even loved…

Loved. She'd told him she loved him. How could she have done such a stupid thing? She jumped up as if the seat had exploded and went near enough to him so as not to be overheard.

"Oh my, Shamus, when I told you I loved you outside, I didn't mean to say that. It's more of a 'really, really like you.' I was carried away by the moment."

"Don't worry about it," he said simply. "I feel the same way about you."

He did? *Really, really like,* she assumed he meant. Gazing into his eyes, she wondered if she was kidding herself about the "like" part. But she shouldn't be worrying about that now.

She broke eye contact to survey their surroundings. More people from the upper floors were pouring out of the elevators and heading toward the front door. A remote control could have set off the bomb from an upper floor, and one of them could be the bomber.

Or maybe not.

"Are we safe here?" she asked.

"I don't know. I don't know that anywhere's safe right now." He led her to a corner where they could watch the room better and be less conspicuous to anyone coming inside. "I do know you saved yourself that time. Trying to put me out of a job?"

Mallory's laugh sounded strangled. "Not really. I guess I'm just getting used to bad things happening. Isn't that horrible?"

"Yeah." He wanted to kiss her, to reassure himself she was

really all right, even though a kiss would be stupid for a couple of reasons.

"I'll find the guy, Mallory, I promise. This isn't going to continue."

She looked back at him with such trust in her green eyes that he felt a familiar surge of fear. He wanted to tell her he was wrong. Not to count on him. He'd already gotten Ruth killed. But he couldn't say a word.

She needed him to fight.

His phone rang, and Mallory jumped. He didn't recognize the number on the screen, which, in the day of throwaway phones, didn't mean much. It could still be someone he wanted to talk to.

Like the bomber. Or Ethan.

He tapped the button. "Yeah?"

"Stop seeing her, Burke. Your only warning. Next, she dies."

TWELVE

Shamus clenched his teeth so he wouldn't ask the caller if he wanted his jaw broken. By him. Or a number of other suitably nasty punishments he could think up. "And whom would this be?" he asked, and got no response.

Shoving the phone in his coat pocket, he met Mallory's gaze, and she lifted her eyebrows in question as she stood.

"The bomber," he admitted.

"I didn't think it was your mother," she told him.

"You're right. If Mom didn't like my choice of friends, she would have blown up my car, not yours. How serious were you when you said it was war earlier? Any chance of you flying off to some faraway vacation spot like the Bahamas for at least a week so you'll be safely out of my way? I'll pay."

"Wow. A ticket to Aruba versus snow in Indiana with bombs going off? Any normal female would say yes."

"But you aren't normal?" he said.

"Nope. I'm angry. That's not normal for me." She stopped the bantering. "The bomber threatened me, didn't he?"

Shamus's black-velvet eyes lost their softness. "Yeah. I'm supposed to stop seeing you, or you're dead. The SUV was the last warning. I want you to leave town."

She backed up from him. "I'm not going, Shamus." The

bomber would love for her to abandon Shamus, and she wasn't about to. "We have a teenager to find."

"We can't work together. I need to find Tara to get to the bomber, and if he sees us together, he might shoot you. Or me. I have the experience, Mallory. You need to let me handle it."

She considered his words. "I'll think about it. If you will go outside to talk to the cops for me. If Dickerson is out there and I have to talk to him one more time today, I might explode all on my own."

"I will. If you won't sneak off on your own."

"I'll try." That was as good as he was getting. Turning, she headed toward the metal detector and the returned guard and, after that, the staircase leading to the basement.

Shamus swore under his breath. He did care about having his life back again—he'd realized that this morning when he'd been saved from jail by Santa Claus. He'd find the menace who had just called him, and he would get his life back on track, especially with God.

After that…Mallory? Their relationship would need to end. For both their sakes.

Hauling in a deep breath, he headed toward the door to talk to the detective in charge out there. He hoped it was Sullivan, the one cop he was sure would let him see the surveillance video from the lot, so he could find out who had planted the bomb in Mallory's car.

And then his fight would begin, and, God help them both, Mallory would see what he would become.

Find Tara Tripp. All afternoon, the thought kept reoccurring to Mallory, like a computer reminder that she kept dismissing only to have it pop up ten minutes later. She couldn't figure out why she couldn't shut it down. Shamus was taking care of everything. He'd even brought her his truck so she would have transportation, telling her where he'd parked it in the lot and dropping the keys into her hands. He'd gotten the afternoon off to investigate the bombing. So why the nagging feeling she should be out there doing something to find the very person Shamus was already hunting for?

Maybe it was the anger that was still thrumming through her veins, making her want to act. The bomber had blown up her car. He'd threatened her life. And he was ruining all the good she'd done in Shamus's life.

Or rather, that God had done. She'd take full responsibility for her anger, but she needed to give God the credit for her successes. The more angry she let herself be, the further she felt from God. It had to stop, and all she knew how to do was pray. Which she did, but the refrain came back.

Find Tara Tripp.

Her cell vibrated. Shamus.

"We're pretty sure we know who the bomber might be, princess," his voice rumbled in her ear. It made her feel good just to hear it, even if he was back to calling her *princess.* "One of my probationers was seen in the parking-lot surveillance footage, planting something on your vehicle. A twenty-four-year old named Cal Johnson I revoked for assault, so it looks like the motive was revenge. There was already a warrant out on him, and now we have a description of his vehicle. I'm going out with Detective Sullivan shortly to try to find him."

Where was her surge of relief?

Oh, yeah. "What about Tara?"

"At this point, she's irrelevant."

But she wasn't. Not to Mallory. Putting that aside, she took a deep breath. Her eyes rising to make sure no one was paying attention, she asked softly, "What about you?"

"I was considering going back into the SFPD. At least there, my coworkers know the risks. And you'll be safe."

"So it's over?"

"Yeah. It's over."

Her voice almost caught, but she forced herself to speak. "I'll be seeing you again from time to time."

"I have to give two weeks' notice."

He didn't go beyond that. Then neither would she. It was over.

Or maybe it had never really begun. Maybe it had just been the danger that had pushed them into each other's arms.

But if that was so, why did the loss of Shamus feel so painful?

Shamus was gone, so she hung up the phone.

Now what? She stared across the room at Tony and Jessica, neither of whom had spoken to her since she'd entered the office that afternoon. Mosey hadn't, either, before he'd gone to court. She no longer trusted Ginny.

She had nothing left.

Except God. She needed to get close to Him again. Get back the joy of being in His presence. Only she wasn't sure how to do that anymore. She was too angry over losing Shamus.

Find Tara Tripp.

The urgency struck her again, full-fledged. If she could just do that, she wouldn't find joy, but maybe she could get some peace from the nagging in her brain.

Tapping on her computer keys, she searched for and found what she thought might be the home phone number of Tara's friend Alexis, the one who refused to give any information at the interview. She probably wouldn't return her call voluntarily, but a well-worded message on her parents' phone instead of the teenager's cell might get one of them worried enough to make her call back.

The phone rang at four-thirty. Bingo.

"Why are you calling me?" Alexis said without preamble once Mallory identified herself and the office. "My mother is really mad. She thinks I'm in trouble."

"I need to know where Tara Tripp is, Alexis. I have some money for her because of her father's death."

"No way. Tripp didn't have any money in his account, and he wouldn't leave her any insurance. He just wouldn't."

She was prepared for the girl's suspicion, but the certainty behind Alexis's reason for refusing had her puzzled. "How do you know that?"

"He wasn't who everyone thought he was—let's just put it that way," she said impatiently. "Is there anything else?"

What on earth did she mean? Mallory decided not to worry about it for the moment.

"Alexis, I need her address. The money didn't come from her father. It was donated by people who care about her and want to make sure she has enough to live on." Only the word "people" was a lie, and since this was life or death, she prayed God would forgive her. She was the only person, but she did have money to give Tara to help the girl out, if she could just find her.

"How much money we talking?" Alexis asked.

"Five hundred."

"I'll get back to you." Alexis hung up. Hoping it would be enough to entice Tara out of hiding, Mallory replaced her phone in its cradle and started typing an update on one of her probationers.

Patience.

Bess came out of her cubicle and cleared her throat.

"Announcement for those of you who are still here."

Mallory did an inventory. Tony and Jessica, and now Ginny, who was just walking in.

"The new wing of offices we were promised a year ago is finally ready. They're moving the furniture Monday, so work from home and report upstairs on Tuesday."

Bess disappeared back into her office space as Jessica gave a delighted whoop. "Yes! No more basement." She slid her chair over to Tony, and, after a quick, whispered conversation, the two rose. Tony got up to get his jacket and tossed Jessica hers, then quietly asked Ginny to join them to celebrate the move upstairs, where they would get their own offices. Ginny refused, which took Mallory by surprise. Apparently Tony, too, from the confused look on his face.

She checked her watch as Jessica tried to change Ginny's mind. Five o'clock. Quitting time. She'd give Alexis a few more minutes. She hadn't given the girls her business card when she'd talked to them last, so they didn't have her cell number. If she called the Willoughby home again, she might get accused of harassment, and then she'd have to explain herself to Bess—or, worse, Detective Dickerson. No, thanks.

The phone rang just as Ginny started walking toward her desk. Mallory scooped up the phone, held up her hand for Ginny to wait and started to give her usual greeting.

"I haven't got that long," Alexis said abruptly. "Tara said bring the money to their old rental by six o'clock, but not to bring the other officer with you. She's not going to foster care, she said, no matter what. She also said you know the address. And don't bother me again." She hung up.

Mallory hung up, too, and turned off her computer. Fighting traffic would be horrendous at five o'clock on a Friday a week before Christmas—she needed to get going.

Grabbing her purse, she rounded her desk, and there was Ginny, looking at her with red-rimmed eyes.

Mallory had forgotten she was there.

"I'm so sorry I've been rotten to you," Ginny said, her negativity gone. "I want to explain what's been going on."

"Sure, but I can't right now. I have to be somewhere. Maybe you could come over tomorrow. Call me." Guilt immediately hit her, but she shoved it aside, just as Ginny had shoved their friendship aside. Walking past her, she reached for her jacket.

"It was Ethan," Ginny continued as if she hadn't heard what Mallory said. "He asked me to do whatever it took to get you not to look for Tara."

He what? And he had let Ginny know he was back, but not his own sister? Mallory's handbag almost slipped through her fingers. Ethan had told Ginny to turn on his own sister and her best friend? And Ginny had obeyed?

And now she expected her to just smile and accept it all? She would have, just a couple of days ago. But now? Now she wasn't sure what to say or do. She ought to pray, ought to be nice—but where was the sense in that? Shamus was right. People just walked all over you.

"And now Ethan's disappeared," Ginny said. "He said not to contact anyone if that happened, and I don't know what to do."

"Do what I would do, Ginny." Mallory walked over to Shamus's desk, took one of his cards from the holder and put it in Ginny's hand, pressing her fingers closed around it. "Call Shamus."

Hurrying out of the office, she bolted up the stairs. She couldn't believe this. Ginny had known Ethan was back in the city and hadn't told her. She might even have known Ethan had been following her dressed as Santa, although her brother might well have kept that from Ginny. Who knew? Shamus's cynicism over people was well-founded.

Stop worrying about them, she told herself. Focus on Tara.

Shamus's truck was his second vehicle, he'd told her, a gorgeous, deep green Ford. New. It kind of matched her eyes. Mallory hoped the bomber didn't see her driving it and blow it up, too.

For a few seconds she considered taking a cab instead of risking Shamus's wheels, but she didn't have the time to wait for one after listening to Ginny. Instead, she cautiously drove to the bank, then to a convenience store to buy herself a cup of coffee. Twenty minutes later she pulled up at the head of the street that the Tripp rental was on and cut her lights.

To one side of her was a house for sale and to the other, across the street, a lot with no house, but lots of trees, overgrown brush and a small, rusted shed. She could scope out the situation from there to see if she would be safe enough without arousing suspicion.

At the former Tripp rental, light was glowing white through the windows. A van was in the driveway, and she could see a female, in jeans and a short jacket, carrying a box out and putting it in the open van.

She had found Tara. The neighbors had lied about her squatting there. The neighbors, Ethan, Ginny—didn't anyone care about the truth anymore?

Making a decision she'd been putting off for a little over an hour, she took out her cell phone and tapped out Shamus's number. He answered on the first ring.

"What's wrong?" he asked.

"Nothing. I just wanted you to know I found Tara. She's been squatting at the old Tripp rental."

"Where are you?"

"About three quarters of a block away from her. I've seen her go in and out already. I think a friend is helping her move."

"I'm on my way. Don't you dare confront her alone."

"I have to, Shamus. You won't be able to follow me around forever, and it's time I started taking care of myself."

He made a funny noise she'd never heard from him before. Kind of choked-sounding. "Just stay put."

"I can't." She really would like to do as Shamus asked, but Tara was bringing a suitcase out of the house. No telling when she planned to leave. It could be the second the clock turned six, the hour Alexis had mentioned. "She's loading her van up with her things, and I think she might be changing hiding

places. I need to help her before she disappears again. I just
called so you would know I found her."

"What kind of van?" Shamus asked, just as she pressed
disconnect.

She then turned the phone completely off so she wouldn't
feel it vibrate and tucked it into her outside pocket. She needed
some uninterrupted minutes to talk to Tara before Shamus and
the police arrived. Because Shamus would call the police, she
knew he would. Tara was a witness and could identify the
bomber, at the very least.

She ought to pray first for God's protection before she approached Tara, she knew that. But the words wouldn't come.
She was just too angry. If she could just see the reason behind
all that had happened in the last week, maybe she wouldn't
be. But God had taken her friends, and worse, dangled love
in front of her, love she couldn't have. And for what? For her
to give five hundred dollars to a teenager who was begging
her *not* to help her?

Talk to Tara Tripp.

With a sigh, she checked all around her for anyone who
might be following her. Seeing nothing, she drove down the
block and pulled in behind the van in Tara's driveway.

At the sound of the Ford's engine, the teenager swung
around, but stayed far enough back so she could bolt if she
had to. Mallory couldn't figure out why, since Tara was expecting her to come, but then she remembered she'd driven
her SUV before when she'd come to Bud Tripp's home visit.

Mallory switched off the Ford's lights, got out and moved
to where Tara could see her over the hood. She'd parked too
close to the van to go around the truck in front, so she waited
for Tara to round the van and join her.

"You weren't followed, were you?" Tara asked. The nearby
streetlamp cast a yellow glow over the teenager's dark blond

hair and big eyes. She looked vulnerable as she gazed up and down the street.

"Not that I know of." Mallory pointed to the van. "Where are you moving to?"

"Anywhere but here. Do you have my money?"

"Yes, but I need to know a couple things first. What can you tell me about your kidnapper? Hair color, height, where you were kept, how you got away?"

Her eyes got huge. Fear was so strong on her face, Mallory wondered if the bomber had abused her physically, and her heart melted for the girl.

"Tara, it's okay. I wasn't followed." She was relatively sure of that. "You're safe."

"No, I'm not. If I tell you who he is, and he goes to trial, I'll have to testify against him, and he'll find a way to kill me."

Time seemed to stop. "You know who the bomber is."

Tara backed up, nodding, practically in tears.

"Hon, you have to tell me. He kidnapped you and he killed your father. He also bombed the probation building and my SUV. As long as he's free, he could still hurt someone else."

A trace of confusion swept over Tara's features and was just as quickly gone. "He won't hurt anyone else. I'll be fine. Please, just give me the money and go."

Mallory couldn't do that. She tilted her chin toward the rental. "How did you get the lights and the heat turned on?"

"I have lanterns, and there's a fireplace. If you lied about having money just to ask me questions, I need to leave." She turned and started walking toward the dark, gaping hole of the open garage.

"Wait!" Mallory couldn't let her go, and she didn't even understand why, since the girl was obviously not about to tell her anything. "I wasn't lying about the cash."

Free money being an instant attention grabber, Tara turned. Mallory dug in her handbag, took out the cash and held it up.

Tara double-timed it back to Mallory's side, folded the bills and stuffed them into the pocket of her tight jeans. "Thank you. I've got to finish loading the van, so *please* go."

"I can't." Mallory glanced up and down the street and saw no signs of Shamus or the police. She still had a couple of minutes at least. "I promised your dad I would help you before he died. Please let me keep that promise. You can stay with me at my apartment. I have a sofa bed."

All emotion left Tara's face at the mention of her father. "I'm sorry you went through all this trouble for him, Ms. Larsen," she said flatly. "Bud Tripp wasn't worth it, and he was no kind of father. Believe me. You can go home now confident you did everything you could."

Had she? But why was Tara talking about her father as if he were a stranger?

Ask her. There was no voice, just the firm knowledge that she couldn't let this drop. Something had made Ethan want her to stay away from the girl, and every instinct told her she needed to know what that something was.

"Tara! Wait," she called to the girl's back as she walked toward the garage. "I have more money I can give you. Just talk to me."

Tara stopped at the front of the van and waited for Mallory to join her. The closer she got to the garage, the darker the shadows around her became. God would protect her, Mallory knew, but that didn't mean she could relax her guard.

"I'll give you another hundred if you'll tell me why you think your father—"

A sudden noise inside the garage made Mallory jump. She gazed inside its depths, but all she saw was blackness.

"Is someone in there?" she asked.

"Probably just a neighborhood cat," Tara said with a toss of her shoulders. "You need to go."

A can crashed inside the garage. That was enough for Mallory. She grabbed Tara and pulled her a few feet toward Shamus's truck, but the girl yanked free and ran back to the garage, right into a cuddle with a tall, slim guy Mallory had never seen before. Not that she could see him all that well in the dim light. But she could see a gun.

She could always see guns.

The bomber? No matter—the guy had a gun, and she was done with guns. She put her hands in the air, hoping if Shamus or a cop was nearby, either would see she was in trouble.

"You're not going anywhere, unless it's with us to the cash machine." The tall, thin guy she assumed was Tara's boyfriend and the owner of the van waved his gun.

"You were supposed to stay inside until she was gone!" Tara moaned.

"I told you, we've got to get out of here fast. You were taking too much time."

He pointed the gun higher at Mallory. It was sort of like the day Tripp came into the probation office, all the gun-waving, only it wasn't. This guy looked like he knew what he was doing, and Shamus was nowhere to be seen.

She was in big trouble.

"We want the money you just promised Tara," the man continued, "and then we're leaving the state."

Tara didn't look happy about her boyfriend throwing threats. Mallory could use that.

"Tara, you know I want to help you. But in return, at least tell me who kidnapped you. I'm sure the police won't need you to testify, because they can get him on the bombing evidence. But they need a place to start looking."

She made out Tara shaking her head.

"No more talk," her boyfriend said. "Tara, get her purse and then get in the van. You're driving."

With the boyfriend backing her up, Tara walked to her side and pulled Mallory's red velvet handbag off her arm. Mallory considered fighting with her, but even if she won, there was still the gun.

Tara was still facing her when, to the side of the garage, shadows moved. No shots came. Either the bomber had called off his private war, or Shamus had arrived.

She needed to help him. "Fine. We'll go to an ATM and I'll get you all the money you could possibly want," she said. Up to her remaining balance of two hundred and thirteen dollars, anyway. She kept talking, both to keep Tara and her boyfriend's focus on her, and to cover any noise of footsteps they might hear once Shamus hit the driveway. "But I'm doing this for you, Tara, because I promised your father."

"He wasn't my father," Tara said.

Mallory frowned more deeply. Maybe her denial was post-traumatic shock over Bud Tripp's death, but the girl wasn't acting like she was in shock. She was acting like Bud Tripp really hadn't been her father. Why?

"In the van already." The boyfriend waved his gun again.

She needed to give Shamus and the uniformed officer with him a chance to get to safe cover before Tara's boyfriend turned and was able to spot them.

"Just one question," she said. "What are you going to do with me after I get money for you?"

"Whatever it takes."

Oh, that didn't sound good. Mallory's stomach plummeted, and her gaze flew to the girl. "Tara—"

"Cal will just leave you stranded someplace, don't worry," she said.

Cal? Through years of practice as a probation officer,

Mallory caught herself before showing any reaction. Cal, as in Cal Johnson, Shamus's probationer who'd blown up her SUV? Whom Shamus had implied was the bomber? Who also must have shot Tara's father? Had Tara known that was going to happen? No wonder the teenager had been certain no one else would be hurt—she and Cal were leaving the state.

But something didn't make sense. Tara had also stated her kidnapper would find a way to kill her. Had that been another lie, or was a third person mixed up in this?

"I'm glad you have such trust in him," Mallory said carefully. "But he's holding a gun on *me*. Doesn't that concern you at all?"

"I have to be free. I risked everything to get out of Bud's house, and I'm not about to go into some foster-care place."

Tara risked everything to get out of Tripp's house? Then she'd set up her own kidnapping? A wave of anger swept over Mallory. Everyone had warned her, and she'd just gone her cheerful, trusting way and lost her friends and almost lost her job to keep a promise that didn't even matter.

How could doing what the Lord wanted backfire so badly? She tried to do what He had said—be joyful and caring so people would be attracted to Christ, and obey God's direction in helping both Shamus and Tara. And what had happened? Everyone at work and the people at church had just thought her a fool. Even Shamus hadn't understood why she'd been so trusting and forgiving. So where had any of this gotten God?

Good thing He knew what He was doing, because she sure didn't.

Cal walked toward them. "Get going to the van."

Since the vehicles were bumper-to-bumper, the only way to get to the van's side door would be to go around the rear of Shamus's Ford. Right before Mallory turned to do that, she saw Shamus and a uniformed officer slip to the front of the van and duck, once again out of Tara and Cal's sight. Logic told her neither of them wanted to have a standoff and risk bullets flying in the neighborhood, so they must be planning to take Cal from behind.

The second her hand touched the frigid steel of the truck, a way to give the cop and Shamus the advantage occurred to her. She slipped both her hands into her pockets as if warming them, then waited till she reached the sidewalk, where she spun around, startling both Tara and Cal, who jerked his gun up at her.

"If we're taking the van," she said, "someone's going to have to move the truck."

This close to the streetlight, Mallory could see the "Oh, yeah" moment in Cal's eyes. He waved his weapon. "Tara, get her keys and back it out."

While Tara dug in Mallory's purse, Mallory drew Shamus's truck keys out of her pocket and flung them as hard as she could into the next yard.

Tara cursed, dropped Mallory's handbag and ran after them. In the split second Cal's gaze followed his girlfriend, Mallory grabbed her chance. She rushed to the other side of the truck and ducked.

"Clear, Shamus!" she yelled. What made her say that, she didn't know. Too many police shows, maybe.

Someone yelled, "Freeze, Johnson!" In seconds, she felt thumps against the other side of the truck, making it move slightly, and she peered over the upper edge of the truck bed. Shamus was cuffing Cal. From the look on his face, she thought he might want to cuff her, too.

Well, he couldn't be any more angry with her than she was with herself for approaching Tara without waiting for him. For not trusting his way of doing things—after all, he'd been a cop.

To her right, two patrol vehicles rolled up, blue lights flashing. A portly cop in his fifties she remembered seeing at Tripp's shooting took over custody of Cal, and from the other vehicle, a female officer headed toward where Mallory could see a third cop holding Tara.

It was time to face Shamus.

Rounding the truck, she found her red velvet handbag where Tara had dropped it, picked it up and brushed the dirt off it. Shamus was only a few feet away from her, talking to the newly arrived female officer, who had a handcuffed Tara in custody. She looked around for Cal Johnson and saw he was in one of the patrol vehicles, with the two male officers talking to him.

"Mallory," Shamus said, "we're taking Tara inside."

That couldn't be procedure. More than likely, the officer was a friend of Shamus's and she was allowing him to do some quick questioning on his own. She wanted to be in on that.

They rushed Tara toward the house, but she remembered Shamus's truck keys she'd thrown to cause the diversion. She hurried across the yard, into the next, and found the keys easily in the bright lights from the police cruisers.

The same bright lights that could make her a target if Cal and Tara hadn't been working alone. She didn't feel comfortable until she was inside the front door of the rental.

The small front room was filled with old furniture used by countless renters. Shamus seemed to take up most of it. She moved closer until she was next to him and looked at the female officer's name tag, illuminated by the still brightly burning fireplace and the electric lantern lights. Officer Devlin. The woman would be in Shamus's "new" old life he was running back to at the Shepherd Falls Police Department. Mallory didn't exactly feel jealous. Just sad.

"Sit, Tara," Shamus said. He lifted one of the lanterns to put on the side table next to the teenager, whose face was set on stubborn.

Mallory hoped Shamus could get through to her. She wasn't in the mood to listen to more denials. Tara had been worried about no one but herself, hadn't tried to warn Mallory that she had a boyfriend with a gun around. All the compassion she normally tried to feel for someone who had wronged her was gone, replaced by the burning of anger in her heart.

"You're going down for attempted kidnapping, Tara," Shamus said.

Tara shook her head smugly. "Nope. I told Ms. Larsen to go before Cal got stupid. More than once. Not my fault. None of this is."

"That's not what your boyfriend said. He knows if he gets convicted on this one, he's a three-time loser and he's never getting out. He'll turn on you in a second. Hear that? He won't be charged and you're going into the worst detention you've ever had until you're twenty-one, and maybe even after."

Mallory knew Cal Johnson's probation for his previous offense would be revoked, and he'd go to jail no matter what. But maybe Tara didn't know that.

The teenager seemed wise to the facts. Her eyes defiant, she said, "I don't believe you. Cal wouldn't do that. He loves me."

"Sure he loves you. Enough to blow up an SUV? Are you certain there wasn't more in it for him? Did he tell you about the roll of money he had stashed on him?" Shamus was working from a hunch, made from his long experience as a detective.

Tara's face went red with anger as she called Cal a name. "He swore he loved me. He said he did all of this for me."

"He's on his way to the station for a statement. Are you sure you trust him to take the blame? What else has he been hiding from you?"

"I never want to see Cal Johnson again as long as I live." Her cheeks still red, Tara looked at each of them, her gaze coming to rest on the female officer. "Can I try to make a deal, too?"

"Sure," the officer responded with confidence, not spelling out what Mallory already knew—that trying wasn't the same as actually getting one.

"Okay, then," Tara said, nodding. "I'll tell you everything."

THIRTEEN

Officer Devlin reminded her again she could have a lawyer first, but Tara shook her head.

"Start with why Cal bombed the probation building," Shamus suggested.

"He didn't."

"Tara," Shamus said warningly.

"He didn't! The guy who bombed the building and kidnapped me is my science teacher at Shepherd Falls High."

That was why Bud Tripp had told her to go to Tara's school, Mallory realized. Not to see Tara's friends—but because the bomber was a teacher there. Tripp must have found out who he was—which was why he was murdered.

"He overheard me saying to Alexis about how Bud wouldn't let me see Cal, had even gotten himself arrested while trying to get me away from his influence. The teacher got me aside and offered to set Bud up to be arrested, which would make his probation be revoked and then he'd go to jail. I'd be free to disappear with Cal. All I had to do was pretend to be kidnapped to make it realistic. Only then he really did kidnap me, because he was afraid I would tell who he was."

When Shamus didn't ask another question, Mallory shifted

her gaze from Tara to him. His jaw was clenched, and his eyes were focused on Tara. He looked like he was in shock.

He looked like he knew who she was talking about.

Mallory set her eyes back on Tara. "What's this teacher's name?"

"Paul McCauley."

Shamus's former father-in-law? Mallory's gaze flew back to Shamus, who stood there with his eyes closed and his lips moving ever so slightly.

He was praying.

It had to be true then, even though she could hardly believe it herself. Paul was an elder in the church. He had organized the cantata. He claimed to love God. And Shamus had been married to his *daughter.* Why on earth would the man want to punish him like this?

Shaking her head to clear it, she tried to think of something to say to Shamus. But what? God meant everything for good? How could any of this situation ever be good?

His face grim, Shamus took out his cell phone, called Detective Sullivan and told him who Tara said the bomber was. Then he hung up and turned back to Tara.

"Why did McCauley kill your father?"

"He wasn't my—" Tara stopped and shook her head. "What's the use?" She sighed. "All I know is that Alexis called Bud to find out where I was Friday night, 'cause I was supposed to call her after the kidnapping and arrest was all over. When Bud said I was still kidnapped, she told him what was going on 'cause she heard about the bombing and was scared Mr. McCauley would hurt me."

Tara took a deep breath. "Bud must have called Mr. McCauley at home and threatened him is all I can figure. Mr. McCauley never said a word about killing him to me."

Shamus's jaw moved from side to side. "Why did Cal Johnson blow up Ms. Larsen's vehicle?"

"Mr. McCauley said he'd let me go only if my boyfriend stayed on call in case he needed some help. After he let me go, Cal wasn't going to, except when you told me he killed Bud we decided to do what he said and get away as soon as we could. First he told Cal to beat up some guy. I didn't pay much attention."

Mallory turned to Shamus. "Luke Cramer."

"Had to be." Shamus nodded in agreement. "Cal must have been the guy in the van outside the Second Chance Paul gave my scarf to." He turned back to Tara.

"And then what?"

"Blow up the SUV."

At least things were making sense now—as much as violence ever could make sense. Shamus's former father-in-law had been outside, maybe getting some air, maybe escaping the mistletoe ladies—who knew? He'd observed Shamus and her through the sliding glass door, enjoying each other's company at the party. Then he'd phoned Cal, who'd shown up to get the scarf, find Luke Cramer—who was on foot from what Ethan had said—and set up Shamus.

That explained a whole lot.

Shamus glanced at the female officer. "I'm done."

Officer Devlin nodded. "C'mon, Tara. I don't know what's keeping the detective, but let's go get you processed."

Tara started forward, but Mallory couldn't let her go yet. She had to know one more thing.

"I have a question for Tara." When the other woman nodded, Mallory gazed at the teenager, wanting to drum up some sympathy but finding it extremely difficult.

"You sounded like you didn't think anyone was listening

about Bud Tripp, but I am. Why do you keep saying he isn't your father?"

Tara seemed to melt. "'Cause he's not my father. Back in Minnesota, when I was really little, he stole me and raised me as his daughter, but that doesn't make him my father."

Stole her. Like her sister was stolen. Before she could get carried away, Mallory gave herself a mental shake. Don't trust. Don't trust anyone anymore. She looked up to see Shamus regarding her with narrowed eyes. Except maybe Shamus.

"Is that the truth?" she asked Tara. "Or are you making it up because Tripp wouldn't let you see Cal Johnson?"

"It's the truth. That's why I had to get him locked up, so I could get away and find my real parents. Every time I ran away before, Bud found me. I had to do something."

"Why didn't you go to the police?" Officer Devlin asked.

"I *tried*," she said, exasperation in her voice. "In Minnesota, when I was ten. But he had a fake birth certificate, and I didn't remember what my real last name was, so the cops thought I was lying because I was mad at him, like the story Tripp gave. But I wasn't. After that, Tripp moved us here right away."

"Did he molest you?" Officer Devlin asked, her voice sad. Mallory got the impression she believed the teenager.

"It wasn't like that," Tara said. "He was overprotective and controlling, but he didn't hurt us. He talked like we were really his daughters, so I think he was bonkers. He had to be. Kelly told me he took her because he thought she was in danger, and he stole me so she would have someone to keep her company, because he couldn't let her have friends to talk to. Doesn't that sound cracked to you?"

Kelly? Mallory grabbed Tara's arms.

"How old was Kelly? Where is she now?" More questions lingered in a long line, but she could start with those.

Tara broke into huge tears that rolled down her cheeks unchecked. "I loved Kelly."

Shamus slipped his arm around Mallory's waist.

"Don't be so hard on Tara, Mallory. She didn't kidnap your sister."

Ashamed of herself, Mallory stepped away from Tara and reached into her purse for a tissue. Coming forward again, she gently dried the girl's cheeks and eyes.

"Your Kelly might be my real sister," Mallory told her softly. "I don't know. Could you tell me how old she was and what happened to her?"

"She said she was seven years older than me—according to Bud, anyway."

Seven years would fit. Tara was sixteen, and Kelly would be twenty-three now. Mallory's heart started to pound. "Did she ever tell you her last name?"

"No." Tara's eyes were wide with hope. Mallory could understand that. Someone was finally believing her story. "She couldn't remember much about her past, except she went to the park and then came home, and then Tripp knocked on her door and told her it was the police."

Shamus swore under his breath.

Tara went on. "Kelly said Bud stole me when I was in a park. He made her forget her last name somehow, she said, but she refused to forget that Bud stole her out of her kitchen.

"She took care of me, and tucked me in at night. Bud wasn't my father, but Kelly will always be my sister in my heart."

Tears welled in Mallory's eyes. Kelly had taken care of a little girl who must have been scared to death. But who had taken care of her? Who'd been there to mother her?

She took a shuddering breath, barely holding back her tears. She thought she was starting to tremble—must have been, because Shamus pulled her more tightly to his side. She wanted to bury her face in his broad shoulder and cry forever, but she couldn't. There was one last thing she had to know.

"What happened to her, Tara?" she asked.

"Kelly tried to take me to the police when I was nine so I could go home. Bud caught us. The next day she was gone. He said he made sure she was never coming back because… because she wasn't his little girl anymore. He showed me her shirt with blood on it."

The tears started falling down Mallory's face, the same way they were coming down Tara's, and Mallory left the comfort of Shamus's hold. Leaning down, she gathered the hand-cuffed teenager into her arms and just held her.

She wasn't comforting Tara, who hadn't cared if she lived or died. It was more that Tara had been the last one to see her sister alive, and Mallory was hugging her sister goodbye.

She stayed there only a few seconds, though, because she suddenly realized Tripp had once stayed in this house with a young girl he'd kidnapped, and her whole body went cold. Rising and wiping her tears away on the sleeve of her jacket, she headed for the front door, which was open. Strange. She thought she'd shut it. Shamus followed without asking why she was leaving. She was pretty sure he already knew.

Outside, she saw the portly officer—Rooney, she read on his nametag—standing there.

"I was guarding the door. I guess you're done now," he said. One look at Shamus's face had him walking down the steps away from them to join two officers who had shown up while they'd been inside and were now moving Tara's things from the van to their patrol vehicles.

Briefly, she wondered if Officer Rooney had been listening to Tara's questioning, then decided it wasn't important. She handed Shamus the keys as they headed down the steps and toward Shamus's truck.

"You drive," she said. "I'm kind of angry, and I don't want to accidentally total your truck in a ditch or something."

"Thanks for that." He opened the door for her and headed around to climb in the driver's side. "We need to go someplace safe until Sullivan picks up Paul McCauley."

"Gee, and here I was thinking since we worked together so well to get Tara, we might go after him ourselves."

Shamus gazed at her. "You're kidding, right?"

"Don't you want to know why he didn't want you to be happy?"

"Joe will let me know what he says."

Her face softened. "Why aren't you angry at Paul like I am? He tried to ruin your life. He used a very troubled teenager to do it. He made Cal blow up Mom's quilt. And my SUV."

"Don't worry about that." Shamus reached out and cupped her cheek with his hand, not caring that any of the officers going back and forth from the house with the rest of Tara's things could see him do it. "You can have this truck."

His kindness made her remember just how deep her feelings were for him. But she couldn't go there now. She took his hand, squeezed it and then let go. His hand went back to the seat and was no longer on her cheek. Which suddenly felt cold.

"I can't take your truck," she told him.

"Why not? It's paid for." One side of his mouth lifted in a sort of smile. "Think of it as a Christmas gift."

"It's too valuable."

"Not as valuable as my scarf was. It was made from your heart."

"You're calming me down, Shamus."

"Good."

"But I don't want to calm down. There's nothing to replace the anger."

He didn't reply to that, because she was right. The only

thing that could replace the anger was letting go of the guilt, and returning, as best she could, her focus to God. It wouldn't be the same, but that was the point of going through something as bad as this had been, he guessed.

"Where to?" He put the truck in Reverse and waited. "It has to be someplace safe until Sullivan catches up to McCauley."

"How about going to eat?" she suggested. "There should be enough cops at the Steel Diner to make it a fortress."

He nodded. She fell uncharacteristically silent as he backed out of the driveway and headed toward the middle of the city.

"Want to talk about any of what just happened?" he finally asked. "Want to talk, period?"

"Didn't know what you had till you lost it, did you?" She gave him another smile, and this one lasted a little longer.

He knew all right. He'd discovered what he'd lost when he'd been at the side of the garage, his guts tight with fear. Cal Johnson could have killed her. He'd come through for her, rescued her from the danger. He loved her. He'd realized that standing there. She was gutsy and sweet and strong, and she was the joy in his life he never knew he needed as badly as he did now.

On the other hand, Mallory wouldn't have become entangled in his mess if Paul McCauley hadn't made Bud Tripp bring that bomb. She'd be the joy-filled, caring person she'd been for the last several years. But not if he got any further involved in her life. Who knew how many would line up to come after him in the future, and thus put her through this kind of torture, over and over again?

He couldn't do that to her. Look what her standing by him throughout the bomber mess had done to her. The woman sitting next to him was filled with anger, and he was scared she wouldn't be able to overcome it.

He almost hadn't.

"You know," she said suddenly, "after you told me it was over, that you were going after Cal Johnson, I kept getting this urgent feeling I needed to find Tara Tripp. And not to wait. It was almost like I was supposed to be there, stop her from leaving the state and question her about Bud Tripp so I could find out what happened to my sister after she was abducted." She paused. "Do you think that was the whole purpose behind all of this?"

He hesitated a moment. "Maybe. If it brings you comfort, you can trust that it was all part of God's plan for you."

"It does make me feel better that at least she had love in her life after…" She let the thought drop. "If I hadn't persevered in finding Tara no matter what happened in my life, I would have never known that."

"True." He nodded. "And we also wouldn't have found out that Paul was behind the bombings, unless we caught up with Cal and he confessed. But he was near to getting away—except for you."

He slid smoothly into a parking space near the Steel Diner.

"Are you angry, Shamus? At Paul McCauley, I mean?" she asked.

Was he? "I'm not sure. Maybe some part of me is. I reached out to Paul at the first practice, and he still hated me enough to continue his revenge. But I'm going to talk to him when they catch him, and I'm going to forgive him, no matter what his reason was."

Surprise showed in her eyes. "You are?"

"Yes." He would. "Because God would want me to. And for my own healing. Didn't you teach me that?"

"I guess I did. You learned well." Her face brightened a little. "So maybe I made a difference in your life. Helped you. A little. And maybe losing my friends was worth it to find out about Kelly. And I guess I can try to help Tara, wherever she ends up." She gave him a tiny smile. "All that is good, right?"

"Right." Shamus wanted to kiss her. But he dared not. They had no future together, he reminded himself. He ought to hand her off to someone else, like maybe one of his brothers, to keep her safe until McCauley was caught. But he just couldn't. Some of her anger was leaving her, and she seemed fragile, as if one more disaster would snap her in two. He wanted to be there for her.

Even if he was going to be gone soon.

Shamus reached for the truck door, and so did she, but a blaring siren caught their attention, and just as a patrol vehicle blazed past their truck, they heard a second coming in a different direction. That car turned the corner, its red-and-blue flashers lighting up the sky, and followed the first.

Shamus's phone rang.

"This can't be a coincidence," he said. "Maybe they cornered McCauley." He answered the phone, his eyes staying on her, then shook his head.

It wasn't over yet, then. Mallory scanned outside the truck, watching a merry Christmas unfolding for everyone but her and Shamus.

No, wait, that wasn't true. She didn't have to be angry and think that way. She could have a merry Christmas too, because none of what had happened had destroyed her faith. God was in control, always, and she could have joy in her heart over that. Even if Paul McCauley was roaming around, a danger to them both, even if she and Shamus were meant to be apart, she knew God was working everything to His will. She didn't need to be smiling every day, but she did need to have peace and joy in the Lord.

Hadn't God just shown her that?

She gazed back at Shamus, her heart lighter. He wouldn't

have to live his life the way someone else dictated. He could be happy again, because of God working His miracle on Shamus's life.

He hung up, and the worry in his eyes told her it was not good news. He reached out to take her hand in his.

"It's not only not good," she said, "it's really bad, isn't it?"

"I'm afraid it's too late to help Tara after all."

"What happened?" Her eyes grew huge, and she shook her head in denial. "Not…"

He nodded. "Tara and Officer Devlin reached the police station, and Maggie was leaning back into her patrol car to get something when a sniper shot Tara. She died instantly."

Oh, no. Last week, there had been two people around who knew her sister while she was still alive. Now they were both dead. Why?

She was no longer angry. She was now numb. "I don't understand. Why would McCauley wait until she was at the police station instead of when she and I were in her front yard, easy targets?"

"Paul didn't shoot Tara." Shamus's eyes, lit by passing headlights, were grim. "He was already in custody when it happened. Apparently the Tripps had another enemy."

Confusion flooded Mallory. She had so many questions, she didn't know where to begin. She wanted to talk about who might have shot poor Tara, who'd never really had a chance at life, but she also wanted to know about the man who had started all of the events into motion.

"Did Paul say why, Shamus?" she asked. "Why he came after you?"

"He did. But to understand it, I guess I should tell you more about Ruth's death, and why we both blamed me for it."

She gazed into his eyes. "Take your time," she said.

"I think it's better to get it out quickly," Shamus replied. "The evening of the murder, Ruth and I were both signed up as volunteers to clean up the mission dining hall, but I got called to a murder investigation. Ruth still wanted to go, and I promised I would be there to pick her up at closing. She trusted me, and was outside, thinking I would be coming down the road any second, but I was so wrapped up in my work, I lost track of time. The door was automatically locked behind her, so she couldn't go back into the now deserted building. By the time I got there, she'd already been robbed and stabbed. It was too late to save her. Her murderer had been one of my first arrests, out for revenge. Apparently, he'd been waiting for his chance to get back at me."

Shamus fell silent, but then Mallory squeezed his hand. "But none of that was really your fault. Surely Paul knew that."

"He blamed me because he knew Ruth had been after me to quit the force for years. He thought if I had, his daughter would be around today." Shamus let go of Mallory's hand and sighed. "Paul told Sullivan he wanted me to be miserable and alone, just like he was, since Ruth was all the family he had, and I'd ruined his dream of a bunch of grandkids gathered around him in his old age."

"And he waited to do anything until you had a new job, since the whole time you were looking for Ruth's killer, you were already miserable and basically alone," Mallory guessed.

"Yeah. But then I changed jobs and had a chance at a new life, and he couldn't accept that. He knew as long as someone was after me, I couldn't have peace, so when he overheard Tara talking, he cooked up the kidnapping scheme and had Tripp leave a second backpack with a bomb in it in the hallway. After he saw me at the door, thinking we'd both get out, he set it off by remote. He hired Cal Johnson to destroy your SUV, probably because he knew Cal would be seen on the surveillance cameras and that Johnson was not the brightest bulb in the parking lot and wouldn't realize it."

"But the police would see Johnson, arrest him, and surely he'd talk. Wasn't Paul worried?"

Shamus shook his head. "Remember, Johnson and Tara were leaving the state. I doubt if either of them would have gotten an attack of conscience and come back to turn Paul in. They'd only be implicating themselves in the crimes. Basically, Paul had nothing to worry about."

"What about the card threatening me?"

"He claims Cal made it, because Tara thought you'd interfere with her freedom and she wanted you to stop looking for her." He squeezed her hand. "Paul swears he didn't murder Tripp. And we know he didn't shoot Tara."

"Then who did?"

"I don't know." Shamus looked helpless for the first time since she'd known him. "They'll be going through Tara's things and talking to Keisha and Alexis again. Maybe they'll find a clue."

"Is this person going to come after us next?" She'd been starting to relax, but now anger was pouring back through her veins again. "We have to find out, because I can't go on like this, Shamus. Having to look over my shoulder for the next crisis to hit. Now I know how my father felt. One bad thing after another, until it broke him. We have to do something, because I'm not letting it break me."

Shamus slipped across the bench seat close enough to pull her into his arms. "You won't have to worry anymore. After we find out who this sniper is, I'll be gone out of your life. No more crises. You can get back to being you again."

His words were so full of comfort, their meaning took a few seconds to fully register. She pushed away from him and met his eyes. "You can't get out of my life. You're the only good thing in it right now. Why on earth would you do that to me?"

"Think," he suggested in a gentle voice. "How was your life going until I showed up at the office?"

How was it? Really good. But aware of where he might be heading with this, she didn't want to say.

"Mallory?"

"All right, my life was fine until I decided to help you with your personality problem."

His lips curved upward for a few seconds. Then his eyes grew serious again. "And then it got worse when McCauley came after me, and you got caught in the middle."

"By my own choice."

"And now you're officially miserable."

"Well, yeah, but—"

"How bad do you think it's going to be for you if someone else comes after me? I don't want you to have to live your life like this."

"Surely God won't let it happen again, Shamus. How much is a person supposed to bear?"

"That's what I thought the last time." He repositioned himself back behind the wheel. He needed the distance. He couldn't sit there smelling her rose-scented perfume and tell himself he didn't want to be near her, kiss her and have her in his life every day.

"You need a man who can do for you what you did for me. Help you forget the evil instead of subjecting you to it. Help you keep the love of God foremost in your mind. Keep you smiling. I'll never be the man I was, princess, and I can't give you those things."

Shamus shifted, uncomfortable at what he was doing, but not knowing any other way. Mallory wasn't saying anything, and neither was she collapsing into tears.

"But I won't leave you alone until we find out who this sniper is and why he killed Bud Tripp and Tara. It probably doesn't involve you, but I need to know for certain."

Before he could walk away, he meant. Mallory didn't know what to say. He was right. The thought of living every day with the threat of someone else coming after Shamus—after them—sent her into a withering feeling of depression. She'd grown up in a household where gloom hung over everything done and said like a mound of dirt waiting to bury her. She didn't want to live like that again.

But there was one huge problem. She more than really, really liked Shamus.

She loved him.

Shamus couldn't take her silence. "I've got to get with Sullivan. See if we can catch the sniper. Let me take you to my mother's, where you'll be safe."

"No. Not yet." Mallory didn't want to part from him. Not yet. Tomorrow would be soon enough. "There may be a quicker way to catch the sniper. I've been thinking. If we rule out McCauley killing Tripp, and consider the length of time since Tripp embezzled money without any murder attempts, we can probably assume Tripp was murdered over his only other criminal activity—the abductions." She paused. "So who did it, and why?"

"The first people we usually consider in murder cases are the family or lovers." Since there still was a sniper out there, a sense of uneasiness once again filled Shamus at the two of them just sitting there in the truck, an easy target. He'd have preferred to get moving. But he also was getting the idea Mallory wanted to stay with him, and he couldn't deny her anything.

Except forever with him.

"Tara and Cal could have killed Tripp," Mallory agreed, "but then who murdered Tara? Cal was in custody. The only other family members were two older sisters Tripp hadn't seen in years. Not likely suspects."

She gazed at him with pensive eyes. "We need to look at this from a different angle. There were three other girls abducted from this area in the two years leading up to my sister's disappearance. Where are they? Tripp didn't have them, but what if he knew who did? He had a huge conscience—we already know that since he was trying to pay off what he'd embezzled when he got caught. Maybe someone knew about his conscience, and when they heard about the bombing they worried he'd get caught and cut a deal so they decided to kill him off. And Tara had to be killed in case Tripp had confided in her about the abductions."

She was getting somewhere, Shamus could feel it. "Now we just need to know who Tripp was working with before he moved to Minnesota."

"I did his background investigation for his presentence report. No clues there." She took a breath. "But there's someone else who might know something about the Tripps. My brother. He warned me to stay away from Tara. He hid his identity behind a Santa Claus suit. Why do that unless he wanted to hide from somebody he thought was dangerous—like maybe the sniper?"

"It's certainly worth looking into," Shamus said. "But we don't know where he is."

"No, but Ginny might." She filled him in on what Ginny had told her earlier about Ethan. "The trouble is, I'm so angry at both of them I don't want to go there."

"We could drop you at Mom's, and I could go for you," he suggested.

"Ginny was awful to you. Why on earth would you do that?"

He gave her that look again. The one that said he would do it for *her,* and by now, she ought to know that. She finally had someone who cared more about her than himself. And likewise.

"I'll go with you." She would stay with him as long as she could, even if that was only for this evening. They would be apart forever soon enough.

And her heart ached, because there was nothing she could do about it.

FOURTEEN

Shamus couldn't shake the edginess that had been with him from the second he'd found out Tara had been murdered. The feeling he was missing something important, something totally unexpected, and he needed to be ready for it. So he'd unzipped his jacket and had his gun ready to pull the minute he and Mallory had stepped out of his truck in Ginny's parking lot.

And now, up in Ginny's apartment, after finding out Ethan had made his way back there just an hour ago, he was no less uneasy. He didn't think Ethan was the sniper, but stranger things had happened.

Positioned next to the sofa, where he could take in both the hallway and the main door, he rubbed his thumb against his fingers near his privately owned weapon, another Glock. Mallory was seated on one side of the sofa in front of him, facing her brother at the other end, with Ginny in a chair next to Ethan.

Mallory was so glad Shamus was with her, as this was one of the hardest things she'd ever done, talking to her brother without yelling at him. Not even his immediate apology for missing lunch had eased her irritation at him.

"So why did you leave me behind with Mom and Dad,

Ethan? Disappear for years without getting in touch?" All the other questions she had for him paled in comparison.

"I didn't have a choice." Mallory could see the regret in his eyes. It didn't help. "Remember how we said we were going to work together to find Kelly?"

"Yes." Mallory swallowed. He couldn't know yet what Tara had said about their sister's death. She would have to tell him, but not now.

"I waited until I got my own apartment to start the search. That way I kept it private from Mom and Dad so they wouldn't get upset."

That part she understood.

"First, I reread the journal I'd written with everything we heard the cops say when Kelly disappeared, and then I hit the newspaper archives at the library, looking for articles on other child abductions here and in the states around us. When I started searching, Kelly's case was only four years old, so I started asking questions locally about the car I'd seen when I was coming home from the ballpark that day." He looked past Mallory to Shamus and explained, "The car almost ran me over, and that's why I was able to describe it and the driver's face to people."

"The police decided the man driving didn't have anything to do with it, because Ethan was at the little store a mile away when it happened," Mallory added.

"Right." Ethan met her eyes again. "The man was Bud Tripp."

With what Tara had told Mallory, she wasn't surprised. "And when you saw his face during the bombing coverage, you recognized him."

He nodded. "It's what brought me back here from Chicago, seeing him back in the city and hearing he may have been the one to bomb your office. I thought you were the target of the bombing, because of what happened that made me leave

Shepherd Falls so suddenly." Ethan's eyes narrowed at Mallory. "You didn't look surprised to hear Tripp might have been tied in with Kelly's abduction. Why?"

"I'll tell you in a minute." There were too many things she needed to know first, and she had a feeling after she told him what Tara had said, neither of them would feel like talking anymore. "What made you leave the city?"

"I was in a local bar, trying to find the father of one of the other missing girls to give him Tripp's description and see if anyone had seen him. Two men followed me out, got the jump on me, and I ended up pretty battered. One of the two guys told me if I left the area and never came back, they'd make sure you were safe. Otherwise, I'd lose a second sister. I went to the cops, but they said unless I knew who attacked me, they couldn't help me."

"They should have at least gone to the bar to investigate," Shamus said. "Sounds like something was covered up."

"Yeah. To say the least." Ethan sipped coffee from the mug on the coffee table and then continued. "So I left Shepherd Falls. I realized a lone eighteen-year-old kid had no power to find or stop anyone. I also knew Mom and Dad were keeping the best possible eye on you they could, with Dad driving you to school and Mom picking you up. Even if it felt like a prison, you were as safe as you could be there—unless I stayed."

"But why didn't you write me?"

"I wanted to, but then I would have had to explain what happened, and that might have scared you too much."

It would have. She'd only been fourteen. "I guess I can see that. Where have you been living?"

"Chicago. I worked two jobs and got a degree in computer science, then became involved in writing computer software. I earned enough money to hire someone to look for Kelly. But he had no luck. So I went on with my life—until Tripp bombed the probation building."

"So you came here. To Ginny and not to me. Why?"

For the first time since they'd sat down, Ethan seemed to be holding back. So she looked at Ginny.

"We were friends in high school, I told you that."

Mallory nodded at her.

"I ran into him in New York when I was modeling." Ginny picked at the arm of the chair she was in. "He told me what he just told you about why he left and asked me not to tell you if I saw you. When I quit modeling and came back to Shepherd Falls, I…" Pausing, she winced, and then started again. "I had other things on my mind. I didn't have any contact information for Ethan, not even that he lived in Chicago. So it just seemed easier not to bring it up when I started working here."

Ginny met Ethan's eyes, and their gazes held. There was something more between them than just high-school friends running into each other, Mallory thought. But then she'd already guessed that from Ginny's tears when he'd disappeared. That was nice. Maybe now they could be together forever.

She glanced back at Shamus, her heart breaking all over again. He squeezed her hand, but his gaze drifted toward the door. Why?

Ethan turned his attention back to Mallory. "At Tripp's house the first time, I figured you went in there by yourself, and I was checking on you. Ginny had pointed Burke out to me already, so when I saw him, I knew you'd be okay. That's why I ran."

"So you were really hiding your identity because you didn't want those men to see you had returned?" Mallory asked.

He nodded. "Turned out to be the right thing to do. The day Tripp was shot, I saw one of the men who beat me up a block from Shamus's mother's home. I didn't see him shoot anyone, but on the chance he was involved, I reported the tip anonymously.

"Apparently nothing came of it, because today when I was on my way to meet you for lunch, I saw him again. Of course, I followed him. He went to the same bar I was in that time, and a couple hours later to an apartment complex, and then around five, I followed him to the parking lot at the courthouse. He left when you did."

Mallory's eyes widened. "He followed me to Tara's?"

"Yeah." Ethan flexed his hand, and she saw where his knuckles were scraped. "Figured maybe he knew you were looking for Tara, somehow. He parked one street down from her house and came up by the vacant lot where the overgrown bushes were."

She shuddered. The sniper had been right across from where she'd first parked and called Shamus.

"He had a rifle and was taking aim at one of you when I tackled him. I got in one punch before he put his stun gun on me and left me in the snow. I must have scared him off, though."

Mallory drew in a sharp breath. Ethan had saved her life, bought her time to talk to Tara and learn what had happened to their sister. And he didn't even know that yet.

She had to tell him. "Ethan—"

"No, wait, I'm almost done." He held up his hand. "A little while later, I woke up in the brush. I felt woozy, and you had Burke with you again, so I came back here. I had no proof someone knocked me out, and I figured if I charged in there and made trouble for the sniper, I would only end up being arrested." He shook his head.

"It sounds like you know who he is," Shamus said.

"I do. We found out when Ginny ran the first license plate. The car belonged to a cop. Officer Sean Rooney. That's why I couldn't go to the police—I had no idea who might be working with him."

"Rooney?" Mallory turned and looked upward at Shamus.

"Wasn't he outside on the porch during Tara's questioning? He must have opened the door so he could hear."

"I'm guessing he listened to see if Tara told us there was a cop involved with the abductions so he could either flee the state or figure out a cover story. I'll call Detective Sullivan." Shamus whipped his phone out of his pocket, dialed his friend and started telling him what they now suspected: Sean Rooney was the sniper who had killed Bud Tripp and Tara.

"Mallory?"

Her focus left Shamus, and she turned to her brother. His face was filled with pain.

"Did Tara tell you if it was Tripp who took Kelly?" Ethan asked, his voice breaking.

"Yes." Her eyes filled with hot tears. "Tara said Kelly took care of her and was like a sister to her. And when Kelly wasn't Tripp's little girl anymore, he took her away and she never came back."

The tears started flowing down her cheeks, and seconds later, her brother drew her off the sofa and hugged her like he had the night Kelly had disappeared and their worlds had changed forever.

Mallory's anger melted away, and she forgave him. Like her, Ethan had made the best decisions he could at the time, and despite the agony she'd gone through at home, she'd been protected. While she was at it, Mallory made a conscious decision to forgive Ginny, too. Her friend's explanations didn't really matter—but not letting the anger get the best of her did.

Ginny got them all something to eat, and just as they were finishing up, Shamus got another phone call. The conversation was short, as was Shamus's news.

"They just picked up Sean Rooney."

* * *

"So the danger is really over?" Mallory asked Shamus as she leaned against his truck door in the parking lot of her apartment complex. She was cold, but it was after ten o'clock, so she didn't want to invite him into her apartment.

But she also didn't want him to go. He'd said he was leaving the probation department, and it might be the last time she would be able to really talk to him. Be near him.

Be happy.

"They picked up Rooney with a .50-caliber sniper rifle that had been recently fired in his patrol vehicle, with no explanation from him." Shamus nodded. "Between that and Ethan's identification of him, and what I just heard from Sullivan right before we got here, yes, I would say the danger is over."

Logically, Shamus knew that, but his nerve endings were still screaming at him to stay alert. He chalked that up to a long, tense day and wanting an excuse to stay around Mallory. If she was in danger, he wouldn't be able to leave her.

But he had to face it—she was safe now. Rooney had to be the sniper. He couldn't explain his whereabouts when he'd shot Tara, or why dispatch hadn't been able to reach him the whole time he'd been listening to Tara speak or afterward, when he'd ended her life when he was supposed to be on duty.

And minutes before, while Shamus had been driving his own car to Mallory's apartment, following her to make sure she got home safely, Sullivan had called to say they'd searched Rooney's apartment and found some innocent-looking head shots, the type taken at school, of Kelly, Tara and the three other missing girls from before Kelly's kidnapping. Maybe souvenirs to remember the abductions by, no one knew. But it added to the case against Rooney by showing his involvement with the Tripps and the abductions.

Yeah, Mallory was safe, and he was about to make her safer.

"I'm giving my official notice Monday. Normally I'd have to give a few weeks, but since I'm going back to the department, Bess agreed to let me go early."

"It's going to be hard to replace you," Mallory said, her eyes on Christmas lights down the hillside. "And I'm not just talking about work, either."

Shamus reached out and smoothed a lock of her hair that had fallen forward back behind her delicate ear. "I wish I'd never been a cop."

"So do I." There was no way to keep him from walking out of her life, and Mallory suddenly wanted the slow torture done with. Going on tiptoes, she tilted her head to kiss him. Their lips met, and he cupped her face with his broad, warm hands, leaning into the kiss, warming her with feelings she'd never experienced. This was what real love was like, she realized.

Shamus broke away, turned and strode to his car, leaving without looking back.

And that was what loss looked like.

Holding a deep breath to keep from crying, she rushed down several feet of sidewalk and around the concrete wall of the entryway leading to her door. Taking her key from her pocket, she sniffed back tears.

She was in love with Shamus, and she was too afraid of the past to let him know. What if she admitted she loved him and made him hope, and then the next time evil hit, she couldn't take it? She'd almost become like her father after only a week of trouble. What would have happened if they hadn't found Tara and the sniper and this had gone on and on?

A calloused hand slid over her mouth from behind, and a steely arm clamped her arms against her body. She couldn't move. Sheer panic flooded her, and she immediately began to struggle, but whoever had her was no meek Bud Tripp.

"Don't make a sound," he said, saying each word distinctly.

Blood was pounding in her ears so hard she couldn't place the voice at first. She tried to kick backward, but her captor started pulling her, and she stumbled. He hauled her back up.

"I *told* your brother never to come back to Shepherd Falls. I *warned* him to stay out of investigating. I *told* him he was *risking* you."

Mallory kicked again. *Two* men had beaten up Ethan. They'd forgotten about the second man. She was history.

"Your sister wasn't supposed to be with Tripp." The man pulled in a deep breath. "She was supposed to go to a really wealthy family who wanted her and would give her a good life. The other girls did, and they were happy. I told Tripp that. But then I had to go out of town. That's where everything fell apart. Kelly's new family was waiting. They were getting suspicious, and so I asked Rooney to take her right then, and Tripp could take her to the family. I thought it was settled. Next thing you know, Tripp was telling me Rooney talked about going off on his own and selling the kid to someone else maybe not so nice, and splitting the profits just two ways 'cause I was gone, so Tripp took her before Rooney could. He didn't want her to get hurt." He sucked in another breath. "But Rooney wouldn't have betrayed me."

He hauled her a few steps, but she kicked at him, trying to ignore the horror evoked in her by his words.

"Tripp left the city so I couldn't get Kelly back. I gave up the business after that. Too risky. Then your brother came back, and he nabbed Rooney. But Rooney says he found the sniper rifle. He can even explain the pictures he had of the girls—he got them from one of Tara Tripp's boxes. What he can't explain away is your brother's identification."

Mallory couldn't breathe. His voice...

"Your brother needs to leave town again, permanently.

You're the bait to get him. I am not going down for this. And Rooney won't, either, without Ethan's testimony."

He kept talking, but Mallory didn't want to hear any more. The voice…she recognized it, and it made her both sad and sick at heart.

What do I do, Lord? Shamus had prayed for an answer for the first city block after leaving Mallory's parking lot, and this time, he made sure he kept his heart open to an answer.

The traffic light was red, so he stopped. Downtown Shepherd Falls began with the next block, and the first of several sets of red, green and gold lights was strung across the avenue between streetlamps. He gazed up at them, really focusing at the shape formed in the middle of the lights.

A Christmas present.

That made him think of Mallory. She'd been his Christmas gift from God. The Lord hadn't been silent—He had answered Shamus's prayers for help by bringing Mallory into his life. She had pushed and prodded and pulled until he'd faced life again, saw what he was missing and realized he could be happy.

And here he was, driving *away* from her. What was he doing? If he went on with his life without her, he'd be miserable. That would just give Paul McCauley—or anyone who tried to get vengeance on him in the future—exactly what he wanted. To ruin Shamus's life.

How stupid was he, anyway?

Quickly turning the car around in the very next store parking lot, he headed back to Mallory. He envisioned her eyes lighting up, heard the soft way she said his name in his head. She had said she loved him, blurted it out, then rescinded her words, but just a little. If she did love him, would she be willing to take a risk on his staying around? She'd never said.

But that could be his fault. How many of his fears and his

doubts had spilled over to her, making her unable to tell him he was wrong about no future for them?

He had to find out.

Filled with a joy he hadn't felt for a long time, he made a right turn into Mallory's apartment complex, and then another right turn, heading to the side access that would take him around to her apartment. At the corner he looked left.

And saw a man dragging Mallory toward a car. She was yanking at his arm and trying to kick him.

All his instincts had been right. He never should have left her alone. *Never.* He threw his car into Park. Hesitation could mean her life. No time to call for help. Only to yank his weapon out and run down the sidewalk toward them.

He stopped mere feet from the abductor. Sucked in his breath and pointed his Glock. "Let her go!"

The man's head raised up to see where the threat was, and disbelief sizzled through Shamus.

Mosey Burnham.

Seconds passed. Then, deliberately, the man Shamus never would have expected to harm anyone did something else totally unexpected.

He opened his arms and let Mallory go.

Mallory watched from her second-floor apartment window as Detective Dickerson finally finished questioning Mosey and shut the door to the backseat of the patrol vehicle, safely locking the man inside. Shamus had been allowed to listen to the questioning and had promised to come tell her why he'd returned when it was over, if she would just please get out of the cold. Now he headed across the lot toward her entranceway.

Rising, she ran down the flight of steps, flung open her door and threw herself into his arms. He kissed the top of her head, and she closed her eyes for a minute, hugging him.

"Come upstairs and warm up," she said finally, starting to shiver. "I have coffee made. I would have made cocoa, but you just don't seem like that type."

"I'm not. I'll come up, but only to warm up and tell you what Mosey said. It's already late, and I don't want your neighbors getting wrong ideas by my staying too long."

"That's probably best." They took the stairs quickly, and at the top, she rounded the corner and headed toward the coffee machine to pour him a mug. He was seconds behind her, shrugging off his jacket and rubbing his hands together.

He took one of the stools that faced the island separating the kitchen from a small dining area. She pulled a stool over to the other side, wanting to look directly at him as much as she could while she still had a chance.

He sipped some coffee, put the mug down and then reached across the island to take her hand.

"Mosey spilled his guts, most likely because he had quite a bit to drink this evening after he heard Rooney got arrested, and coming face-to-face with a Glock and an attempted-kidnapping charge sobered him up some.

"He told us he went to law school and then had to drop out to work when he got married. He needed money after one of his daughters was born, and for two years up to the time your sister disappeared he ran an illegal, private adoption scam, posing as a lawyer and soliciting wealthy clients whose names he pulled from 'Want to Adopt' ads."

Shamus gave her a few seconds to absorb that as he circled his hands around his coffee mug, warming them. She gazed at him, trying to understand how Mosey had pulled it off.

"There are adoption laws in this state. Why didn't the prospective parents wonder about lack of court appearances and home studies?"

"In a word—Bud Tripp. Tripp posed as the official doing the

home study and told the parents they didn't have to go to court with Burnham, since the home-study paperwork was completed and they'd both signed it. My impression was Burnham made sure the couples he chose were desperate enough not to question him too closely. If they did, he disappeared."

"So Tripp was finding the girls for him?"

"No, Burnham found the girls through the probation files and paid Rooney to pick up the kids for him."

"Through the probation files? But that would mean—"

"Your mother was on probation. The four girls he admitted to abducting were all from low-income to poor families who had someone on probation."

"Mom was on probation?" she asked, her stomach feeling all woozy. She got up to get some ginger ale from the refrigerator. "What on earth did Mom do? She doesn't even get parking tickets."

"She was on six months' probation for shoplifting food for you kids from a supermarket."

Her eyes flew up, and she had to grip the bottle tightly to keep it from sliding out of her fingers. She came back to the table. "If he did a home visit, I don't remember him."

"He said he did, and that's when he saw Kelly. A man with lollipops? You and Ethan both gave yours to Kelly. He waited three weeks before he told Rooney to take her."

"I remember a man with lollipops, but Mom said he was a friend of Dad's. All three of us were sent to play outside, so we didn't hear anything being said." This was awful. She'd known Mosey before? He had to have recognized her name when she came to work there. With horror, she realized something.

"That was how Rooney knew where to find me. Mosey was telling him. He *knew* Rooney was going to kill Tripp and Tara."

Shamus nodded grimly.

"And get this. Ethan's original assault came when Rooney

overheard him asking questions about Kelly's disappearance. He and Burnham decided to run him out of town. Ethan was lucky. Rooney apparently has a violent streak a mile wide. He wanted to shoot Ethan, but Burnham talked him out of it. He said he remembered how fast Ethan had given his little sister the lollipop, and it made him feel funny."

She closed her eyes briefly. That had to be God stepping in and giving Mosey an attack of conscience. "How about earlier today, when Ethan tackled Rooney near the old Tripp house? Why didn't Rooney kill him then? He easily could have."

"Burnham said Rooney didn't recognize him until too late. He claims he wasn't going to kill you, just put you somewhere until after Rooney got set free."

"Oh, that's really logical. Then I'd get free and bring a kidnapping charge on their heads."

"Not to mention what I would do to them." Shamus's half smile helped her get her focus back. "When it comes to logic, though, you're right—both men were a bit short on it. Burnham thought he was doing the girls a favor, giving them better lives. I get the feeling he would have kept doing it, except when Tripp stole Kelly, he worried Tripp's conscience might extend past protecting one little girl to turning them all in, and decided to stop."

"So when Tripp came back to Shepherd Falls, and then came on Burnham's radar with the bombing, he and Rooney decided they needed to kill him to shut him up?"

Shamus nodded. "They didn't know if Tripp had told Tara how Kelly came to be abducted, so they had to do something about her, too, just in case. Burnham was telling Rooney every move of ours he heard."

Poor Tara. She never had a chance at happiness. "But Tara said she was abducted, too, and it had to be a long time after Tripp left town. Why did he take her?"

Shamus shrugged like a man who'd seen everything and couldn't understand any of it. "Burnham didn't know. My guess is Tripp purposely kept Kelly from having friends she might tell about the kidnapping, and she was lonely. So he took Tara as a companion for her. He must have loved Tara, too, to ask you to take care of her. I think he knew who you were by the last name, was sorry and thought in some warped way he was giving Kelly back to you."

Mallory's face crumpled, and she dissolved into tears. Rising, Shamus rounded the island to pull her off the stool and into his arms. She stayed there until the tears ceased.

Pulling away, she walked to the side table near her couch and got a tissue. "Did Mosey keep track of where the other girls went?"

"Unfortunately, no. Dickerson's got to verify all this first, and also contact the FBI. He's going to run the girls' names from the police files against Mosey's old files. If it all checks out, he'll try to get the story to break nationally in the hope that the couples who got the girls will come forward."

Or maybe they would be too worried about being accused of participating in a crime. But she didn't want to think about that.

She wanted to think about Shamus.

"So it's all over now, and I'm safe, and you can tell me why you came back."

The edges of his lips tipped upward, ever so slightly, in that smile he reserved for her. Taking her hand, he led her to the window facing the parking lot and opened the drapes so they could look out.

He nodded, then turned to her. "Tell me what you see," he said.

"A parking lot full of cars and a Dumpster filled with garbage."

"Try again," Shamus urged. "This time pretend I never

started working at the probation department, that Tripp never bombed the building and that none of the trouble in the last several days ever happened. Pretend that you are exactly the way you were then."

"I'll never be like that again," she said sadly.

"Yes, you will. I guarantee it." He drew her hand to his lips and kissed her fingers. "Pretend you're that Mallory, and then look out there and tell me what you see."

She tried to ignore the warmth of his hand around hers and took a deep breath and looked outside…

…past the lot, past the bushes and down the rolling hill they were on, and farther to the new Christmas tree in the square, with its multicolored lights; the green, red and gold lights across Main Street; and the cross on top of her church that was lit up in the night.

"Now tell me what you see," he asked.

"Christmas, Shamus." She turned away from the window and met his gaze, a soft smile forming on her lips. "I looked past the grime of the parking lot and what just happened there, and I saw Christmas."

"Exactly. I saw the same thing you did just now when I drove away, and I realized that you were the answer God sent to my prayers. If I walked away from you, I would be turning down His present to me and letting not only McCauley win, but any other fool who comes along to try to ruin my life."

"That's true," she said, her voice just above a whisper.

"But I can't guarantee there won't be more people coming after me, sweetheart. There's a risk being in my life."

"Um, Shamus, wasn't that you who just rescued me from Mosey down there? I thought it was. If it was you, I'm sure you noticed it's not exactly that safe being around me, either. I mean, I am a probation officer, and you never know who's going to be breaking the law next. And then there's the fact I've made some fairly dangerous friends, like Mosey, and Ginny—she carries a gun, Shamus. How did they ever okay that, what with her temper?"

He gave her a full-fledged grin. "If you want, we can take things slowly. Date for a while and then see if you still really, really like me."

"We can definitely date, Shamus, but probably you should know about my lie that I've already asked God for forgiveness for."

"What's that?"

"That 'really, really like' I mentioned to you?" she said, her fingers intertwining with his. "It's really, really love."

He leaned down and kissed her, a wonderful kiss of promise and hope and Christmas joy.

EPILOGUE

Shamus was scheduled to work a long shift on Valentine's Day, so Mallory and he decided to celebrate it the Saturday before when they could spend the whole day together. Mallory wanted a day to remember, and Shamus said he'd do his best. Ginny thought that might mean a marriage proposal, and told her to be ready, so Mallory found one of the most romantic dresses she'd ever worn in a shop on Holiday Avenue—red velvet with cream lace trim. Shamus even had a suit on when he picked her up in his car. A suit on his Saturday off. Ginny had to right about his proposing.

Mallory beamed at him. "So where are we going?"

"We have to make a brief detour first, but then it's a party on Holiday Avenue."

A party would be a strange spot to ask her to marry him, but she figured Shamus could make it work. She felt a delightful shiver of anticipation. "Who's coming?"

"Your brother and Ginny."

Ethan had moved back to Shepherd Falls a couple weeks before. Mallory assumed he wanted to be near Ginny, although Ginny swore she wasn't interested in Ethan as more than a friend. Mallory thought she was kidding herself.

"Your coworkers are also on the list."

"Including Gloria Danbridge?" A widow in her fifties, she had replaced Mosey, including in being the office gossip. Mosey was still awaiting trial, along with Sean Rooney. No one had any doubt that they, along with Paul McCauley, would be in prison for a long time.

Ethan chuckled at her wrinkled nose. "No, just Tony, Jessica and Bess." He paused for a few seconds, then made a left onto a heavily traveled highway that would take them into the industrial section of Shepherd Falls. "Your parents might be there, too."

If he had invited them, he *had* to be planning a proposal, but her eyebrows lifted skeptically. "Dad's getting better at dealing with people, but he still never goes anywhere."

Shamus glanced sideways at her. "Have faith."

"I do," she smiled. "I have faith you'll make this a 'day to remember,' like you promised."

He grinned at her, his eyes saying she'd be right.

"So where's the detour to?" she asked. They were on the outskirts of town. "All I see are industries and the—"

"Bus station," Shamus said, pulling into the huge lot and driving slowly up to where people milled near the door. "Take a good look. See anyone you might know?"

"Oh, Shamus, you invited my Grandmom Elle!" Mallory's heart pounded with excitement as she peered through the windshield. Her grandmother was the only relative she had left who lived out of town. This had to be her engagement day if he'd gone through all that trouble—

No Grandmom Elle, but someone else she saw made her heart stop. There, next to a woman pushing a supermarket cart filled with possessions, was a young woman with long, wavy chestnut-red hair who looked remarkably like Mallory. Afraid to believe what she was seeing, Mallory's eyes teared up and her lips fell open as Shamus drove into the first parking space he could find and shut off the motor.

"Yes, it's Kelly," he said, because she couldn't speak. "Turns out Tara talked to Officer Devlin after we left that night. She said Tripp had kept Kelly's shirt to scare her with if she tried to leave again. It was found in his belongings and tested. It was fake blood on the shirt, nothing but food coloring and corn syrup. You were right after all. Tripp couldn't kill anyone. He took Kelly someplace safe to give himself time to get away if she eventually turned him in—his older sister's farm in rural Minnesota. Kelly had already moved away, but the woman still had a copy of Kelly's social security number. From that point on, it was just a matter of finding out where she'd been working to slowly track her down." He grinned. "How's that for a day to remember?"

She threw her arms around his neck and kissed his cheek more than once, then turned to fling open the car door.

"There's more," Shamus said, grabbing her arm gently before she got out. She turned back to him, her eyes filled with excitement.

"Will you marry me?" he asked.

"Oh, yes!" Leaning forward, she kissed him again, her tears of happiness falling freely, and then charged out of the car to run toward her sister.

Shamus sat back in his seat to wait and just smiled. His mother was going to be thrilled.

* * * * *

Dear Reader,

As with most of my stories, what inspired me to write MISTLETOE AND MURDER was a situation I found intriguing: How much would you be willing to sacrifice to fulfill a relative stranger's dying request to save his loved one from danger? What if you gave up a lot, only to find out fulfilling the request could make matters worse for the person you were supposed to be saving?

Mallory Larsen felt God-led to respond to that call and to the one to change Shamus Burke's life, and it worked out for her. She found answers and was freed from the guilt lacing her to her past. And best of all, she helped Shamus Burke, a wonderful man who was lost, to find God, and love, again. At Christmastime.

Thank you so much for reading MISTLETOE AND MURDER. I hope you enjoyed it, and that you have a joy-filled Christmas and the happiest of New Year's!

Florence Case

QUESTIONS FOR DISCUSSION

1. In the first part of this book, Mallory believes she should be nice and understanding no matter how people act toward her. She wants to obey what God says in Ephesians 4:31-32. Do you think being tenderhearted toward everyone, and always forgiving, is sustainable? Why or why not? Do you know anyone who is like Mallory was at first?

2. Mallory likes to crochet and knit items and give them to people to make them happy. Name something that made you happy in the last year. Was it something you did for someone, or for yourself, or was it something someone did for you? How long did your happiness last?

3. What kind of joy is really meant in James 1:2? Can someone really be joyful no matter how bad life gets? In the Bible, what is the difference between happiness and joy?

4. What do you think made Shamus act the way he did in the first part of the story—guilt at not putting his wife first, grief over his wife's death or anger at the murderer? Defend your choice(s). Can guilt ever be a good thing for a person? How?

5. Mallory wanted to change Shamus back to how he was in the past, before his wife's murder, by helping him to really connect with people again. Could he have become the way he was? Would he have wanted to be? Why or why not?

6. Do you think Shamus was ready to get involved in a relationship with a new woman at the beginning of the book? What drew him to Mallory during the course of the story, and vice versa? Was it enough to base a solid, lasting relationship on? Explain.

7. Mallory promised a dying man she would save his daughter, who would have no one who really cared if she didn't. Why do you think it was so important for Mallory to keep that promise? If you were asked something similar that tugged at your heart, would you keep the promise no matter what it might cost you? Would you accept the loss of your friends? The loss of love? How much would you risk?

8. Ginny returned Mallory's gift made from her heart in a hurtful manner. Have you ever gone out of your way to make someone a gift or buy them something special, only to have it ignored, laughed at, trashed or maybe given away to someone else? How did you handle the rejection?

9. Can anger ever be good? How? Do you think Mallory was inwardly angry all along? In what way was it good for Mallory to finally admit and show her anger to others as opposed to always turning the other cheek? In what way was it bad?

10. Do you think God works everything together for good? Think of something in your past that didn't work out or was really difficult to deal with. Can you tell what good might have come from it? Does this saying mean we have to feel good about what happened?

11. When did Mallory's anger toward her brother dissolve? How about toward her father? How did realizing God had worked almost everything out for the good change her? Do you think she was living her faith when she was angry?

12. What was Mosey Burnham's real motive for doing what he did? Do you think he really believed the girls were better off, or was he just greedy? Can some people be born without consciences? Or is evil something real? (See Ephesians 6:12.)

*Here's a sneak peek at "Merry Mayhem"
by Margaret Daley,
one of the two riveting suspense stories in the
new collection CHRISTMAS PERIL,
available in December 2009 from
Love Inspired Suspense.*

"Run. Disappear... Don't trust anyone, especially the police."

Annie Coleman almost dropped the phone at her ex-boyfriend's words, but she couldn't. She had to keep it together for her daughter. Jayden played nearby, oblivious to the sheer terror Annie was feeling at hearing Bryan's gasped warning.

"Thought you could get away," a gruff voice she didn't recognize said between punches. "You haven't finished telling me what I need to know."

Annie panicked. What was going on? What was happening to Bryan on the other end? Confusion gripped her in a chokehold, her chest tightening with each inhalation.

"I don't want," Bryan's rattling gasp punctuated the brief silence, "any money. Just let me go. I'll forget everything."

"I'm not worried about you telling a soul." The menace in the assailant's tone underscored his deadly intent. "All need to know is exactly where you hid it. If you tell me now it will be a lot less painful."

"I can't—" Agony laced each word.

"What's that? A phone?" the man screamed.

The sounds of a struggle then a gunshot blasted her ear drum. Curses roared through the connection.

Fear paralyzed Annie in the middle of her kitchen. Was Bryan shot? Dead?

The voice on the phone returned. "Who's this? Who are you?"

The assailant's voice so clear on the phone panicked her. She slammed it down onto its cradle as though that action could sever the memories from her mind. But nothing would. Had she heard her daughter's father being killed? What information did Bryan have? Did that man know her name? Question after question bombarded her from all sides, but inertia held her still.

The ringing of the phone jarred her out of her trance. Her gaze zoomed in on the lighted panel on the receiver and saw the call was from Bryan's cell. The assailant had her home telephone number. He could discover where she lived. He knew what she'd heard.

"Mommy, what's wrong?"

Looking up at Jayden, Annie schooled her features into what she hoped was a calm expression while her stomach reeled. "You know, I've been thinking, honey, we need to take a vacation. It's time for us to have an adventure. Let's see how fast you can pack." Although she tried to make it sound like a game, her voice quavered, and Annie curled her trembling hands until her fingernails dug into her palms.

At the door, her daughter paused, cocking her head. "When will we be coming back?"

The question hung in the air, and Annie wondered if they'd ever be able to come back at all.

* * * * *

Follow Annie and Jayden as they flee to Christmas, Oklahoma, and hide from a killer—with a little help from a small-town police officer.

Look for CHRISTMAS PERIL by Margaret Daley and Debby Giusti, available December 2009 from Love Inspired Suspense.

REQUEST YOUR FREE BOOKS!
2 FREE RIVETING INSPIRATIONAL NOVELS
PLUS 2 FREE MYSTERY GIFTS

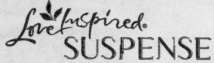

YES! Please send me 2 FREE Love Inspired® Suspense novels and my 2 FREE mystery gifts (gifts are worth about $10). After receiving them, if I don't wish to receive any more books, I can return the shipping statement marked "cancel". If I don't cancel, I will receive 4 brand-new novels every month and be billed just $4.24 per book in the U.S. or $4.74 per book in Canada. That's a savings of over 20% off the cover price. It's quite a bargain! Shipping and handling is just 50¢ per book.* I understand that accepting the 2 free books and gifts places me under no obligation to buy anything. I can always return a shipment and cancel at any time. Even if I never buy another book, the two free books and gifts are mine to keep forever.

123 IDN EYM2 323 IDN EYNE

Name	(PLEASE PRINT)	
Address		Apt. #
City	State/Prov.	Zip/Postal Code

Signature (if under 18, a parent or guardian must sign)

Mail to Steeple Hill Reader Service:
IN U.S.A.: P.O. Box 1867, Buffalo, NY 14240-1867
IN CANADA: P.O. Box 609, Fort Erie, Ontario L2A 5X3

Not valid to current subscribers of Love Inspired Suspense books.

Want to try two free books from another series?
Call 1-800-873-8635 or visit www.morefreebooks.com

* Terms and prices subject to change without notice. Prices do not include applicable taxes. Sales tax applicable in N.Y. Canadian residents will be charged applicable provincial taxes and GST. Offer not valid in Quebec. This offer is limited to one order per household. All orders subject to approval. Credit or debit balances in a customer's account(s) may be offset by any other outstanding balance owed by or to the customer. Please allow 4 to 6 weeks for delivery. Offer available while quantities last.

Your Privacy: Steeple Hill Books is committed to protecting your privacy. Our Privacy Policy is available online at www.SteepleHill.com or upon request from the Reader Service. From time to time we make our lists of customers available to reputable third parties who may have a product or service of interest to you. If you would prefer we not share your name and address, please check here. ☐

Love Inspired®
SUSPENSE

TITLES AVAILABLE NEXT MONTH

Available December 8, 2009

CHRISTMAS PERIL by Margaret Daley and Debby Giusti

Together in one collection come two suspenseful holiday
stories. In "Merry Mayhem," police chief Caleb Jackson
is suspicious when a single mother flees with her child to
Christmas, Oklahoma, where danger soon follows them. In
"Yule Die," a medical researcher discovers her patient is her
long-lost brother—with a determined cop on his tail.

FIELD OF DANGER by Ramona Richards

Deep in a Tennessee cornfield, April Presley witnesses a
grisly murder. Yet she can't identify the killer. Until the
victim's son, sheriff's deputy Daniel Rivers, walks her
through her memory—and into a whole new field of danger....

CLANDESTINE COVER-UP by Pamela Tracy

You're not wanted. The graffiti on her door tells
Tamara Jacoby someone wants her out of town.
Vince Frenci, the handsome contractor she hired to
renovate the place, wants to protect her. But soon they
discover that nothing is as it seems...not even the culprit
behind the attacks.

YULETIDE PROTECTOR by Lisa Mondello

Working undercover at Christmastime, detective Kevin
Gordon is "hired" to kill a man's ex-wife. Yet the dangerous
thug eludes arrest and is free to stalk Daria Carlisle. Until
Kevin makes it his job to be her yuletide protector.

LISCNMBPA1109